Sherryl Clark's first children's book, *The Too-Tight Tutu*, was published in 1997 and she now has more than 40 books in print. Most recently, she has published *Tracey Binns is Trouble* and *Tracey Binns is Lost* and her young adult novel *Bone Song* was published in the UK in 2009. *Farm Kid* won the 2005 NSW Premier's Literary Award and *Sixth Grade Style Queen (Not!)* was an Honour Book in the 2008 CBCA Awards.

www.sherrylclark.com

Also by Sherryl Clark

Tracey Binns is Trouble
Tracey Binns is Lost

one perfect pirouette

by award-winning author
sherryl clark

UQP

First published 2010 by University of Queensland Press
PO Box 6042, St Lucia, Queensland 4067 Australia

www.uqp.com.au

Typeset in 12.5/17pt Garamond by Post Pre-press Group, Brisbane
Printed in Australia by McPherson's Printing Group

The University of Queensland Press uses papers that are natural, renewable
and recyclable products made from wood grown in sustainable forests.
The logging and manufacturing processes conform to the environmental
regulations of the country of origin.

Cataloguing-in-Publication Data
National Library of Australia

Clark, Sherryl.
One perfect pirouette / Sherryl Clark.
978 0 7022 3841 3 (pbk.)
978 0 7022 3806 2 (ebook)
For primary school age.
Ballet – Juvenile fiction.
A823.3

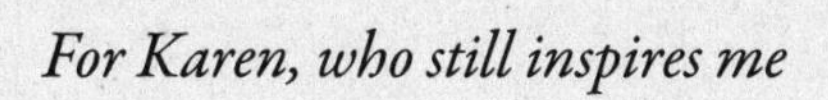

For Karen, who still inspires me

CHAPTER 1

I woke at dawn, my room filled with a strange grey light, the threads of a horrible dream clinging to me like a spider's web. My heart thumped loudly and my legs ached, like I'd been dancing non-stop in my sleep all night. I lay there staring at the cracks in the ceiling, trying not to think, but my brain chimed the word over and over. *Failure. Failure. Failure.*

I flexed my feet, stretched, but the ache still dragged on my leg muscles and I groaned. How could I possibly dance well this morning? Let alone prove how good I was? But it was what I had to do. Right from the first lesson, I had to dance at my absolute best. Because if I didn't, everything my family had sacrificed for me to have my chance would be for nothing. If I failed, I'd have to crawl away and hide – forever. It'd be better than having to face them all across the breakfast table every day and know they were thinking, *She wasn't worth it.*

As soon as I heard someone stirring, I leapt out of bed and dressed in my gym gear, then started warm-up stretches in the lounge, where there was more room. Orrin, my older brother, shuffled past, grunted at me and shut the bathroom door behind him. By the time the family was up and eating breakfast, sweat coated my whole body, but at least I felt less like a stick of wood and more like a dancer. Apart from the hot rocks in my stomach.

I showered and tried to eat, but the cereal stuck in my throat and I scraped it into the bin when no one was looking.

'Clean your teeth and we'll get on the road,' Mum said. I nodded and took a couple of deep breaths, but they didn't help. Best to keep moving and not think too much.

Mum drove me to the Ellergren Dance Studio in our old Holden, and even though it was about twenty minutes from our house, we seemed to arrive in ten seconds. My legs had turned back into sticks and I tried to breathe normally, but I sounded like a gasping elephant.

'Are you all right?' Mum asked.

'Ermmm.'

Our car clanked down the street, past office buildings and a church, and Mum turned into a car park. As we thumped over the driveway entrance, a girl ran across in front of us. Mum slammed on the brakes so hard, we both lurched forward and snapped against our seatbelts. Mum yelled a four-letter word. My hands shook and I clutched my bag harder.

'Not a good start,' she muttered. 'But at least we're here in plenty of time.'

'Mm-hmm.'

She parked and turned off the motor. I climbed out slowly, staring around; our old bomb was surrounded by shiny black and red cars and 4WDs, and the groups of mothers chatting were dressed in the kinds of clothes we wore to weddings.

At least Mum's trackies were fairly new, but she was wearing her old Tweety Bird T-shirt. It shouldn't have mattered – Mum looked like she always does – but suddenly I wished she was in tailored black pants and cool shirt like some of the other mothers.

Focus! This is about dancing!

The front entrance had large wooden double doors between two white columns. We'd been here just four weeks ago for an evaluation session. I remembered the foyer had a black-tiled floor and white walls covered in pictures of ballet dancers. As Mum tried to hustle me past, I'd looked closer and realised they were all of the one dancer – Astrid Ellergren. The woman who was maybe about to change my life.

Mum had rushed on through, dragging me with her, and we ended up in the studio.

'There she is,' she'd whispered, and charged across the floor towards Ms Ellergren. I followed slowly, taking it all in. One wall covered in mirrors, barres along the other side, polished wooden floor, high windows, a piano and a sound system.

As I got closer, I could hear Mum. 'Her previous teacher, Suzanne Calzotti, said she was extremely talented, you see, so we –'

'I know,' Ms Ellergren said. 'That's why I agreed to see her.'

'Oh. Right.'

Mum had been more nervous than I was. Ms Ellergren knew all about me. When Mrs Calzotti retired, it seemed impossible to find another teacher as good, and then Mrs Calzotti put us in contact with Ms Ellergren. The problem was that her school was in Melbourne.

'Hello, Brynna.' Ms Ellergren smiled. 'I'm going to do an evaluation, because I want to make sure you're up to my advanced class before I allow you into it.'

An invisible hand twisted my guts. 'Okay.'

Mum's face dropped. 'But –'

'Suzanne gave Brynna a high recommendation, but there's a lot at stake here.'

'Yes, the National Ballet School audition,' Mum began.

'Before she gets to that,' said Ms Ellergren, 'I need to see what bad habits we have to erase, and whether she's strong enough for this level. She may need to begin in a lower class.'

Mum and I had stared at each other. So I mightn't be good enough to audition for the NBS this year? The invisible hand twisted harder.

'You do know Brynna has already applied to audition,' Mum said.

Ms Ellergren raised her eyebrows. 'You may want to reconsider if she's not ready.'

'But –' Mum was saying nothing. I had to audition. I *had* to!

If Ms Ellergren didn't think I was ready, though . . .

'Have you come with your leotard on?'

I nodded. My voice had left me.

'Get your shoes on quickly, then.' She closed the studio door and waited near the mirrors.

I stripped off my track pants and top, crossed and tied the ribbons on my ballet shoes and stood, praying that my knees would stop trembling.

'Over to the barre. Let's see you go through the positions and then some barre and centre exercises.' She pointed to a chair by the piano. 'You may sit there, Mrs Davies.'

And Mum sat. I didn't dare look at her, because I knew she'd have on her determined face, the one that said, *You can do it. You know you can.*

The trouble was, I wasn't sure I could. What if Mrs Calzotti had taught me badly? What if I had a million bad habits to fix? No, that was silly. *My absolute best – every time.* I focused totally on Ms Ellergren's voice, shutting out Mum and my jumbled worries, and placed my feet in first position.

Twenty minutes later, it was over. Pliés, dégagés, arabesques, tendus and then a check of my hips, legs and feet. Ms Ellergren put my left foot back on the floor and straightened up. 'Good. Suzanne was right. You can join my advanced class.'

Tears filled my eyes and I blinked hard. 'Thank you.'

One rare smile. 'You mightn't thank me after the first class. You have a definite problem with your shoulders and arms that needs to be worked on. They're not in line properly. I believe your application to audition for the National Ballet School has already gone in?'

‘That’s right,’ said Mum.

‘Hmm. We’ll see how you go, Brynna. If you apply yourself, I’m sure you can overcome it. I’ll give you additional exercises and I’ll see you in class.’

Her words had sent an icy spike through me. Shoulders and arms. A problem? What if I couldn’t fix it? Some aspects of bad technique stayed with you forever. Mum had looked at my face and squeezed my arm. ‘You’ll conquer it, Brynnie, I know you will. Now we need to get you to that class.’

Up until then, I hadn’t thought about how I’d attend Ms Ellergren’s school – just that it probably meant lots of travelling. Then Mum and Dad announced that we were going for broke and moving the whole family to Melbourne. We’d been in chaos for the past two weeks, packing, moving, trying to get used to the grotty little house we were renting. Orrin seemed happy about moving, but Tam had turned snarly and bad-tempered. We’d only been in Melbourne two days and he got into an argument with some boys at the milk bar in the next street. He said they’d made fun of his army disposal boots. I knew he was missing his mates and being able to ride his bike down to the creek or through the bush, and I felt awful for him. But Mum said he’d soon get used to it, like we all would.

And now here I was, at the first class.

Mum winked at me. ‘Pick you up later,’ she said. ‘Do your best!’

I raced in to the changing rooms, off the foyer, and

had to battle my way through a crowd of girls in leotards and tights, all heading for the studio. I kept my head down, and found a few centimetres of bench to sit on, then shoved my clothes into my bag. My ballet shoes were worn and a bit tight, but they'd got me through so far. I tied the ribbons, smoothed back the tendrils of hair that had escaped from my bun and rushed into the studio, just as Ms Ellergren was instructing everyone to line up along the barre. I scored the last spot. Suited me. I'd be anonymous there and could get used to the class without looking like an idiot. Although I'd passed the evaluation, the others would probably be far more polished than me.

Music came from a black piano. We drilled in pliés, through each position, going over and over them, while Ms Ellergren walked up and down, correcting everyone a millimetre at a time.

'Hands are not claws, Lisa. Your feet are not floating boats, Ellie. Control them. Tina, head up.'

As she came closer and closer, my face grew hot and sweat trickled down the side of my neck. Then she stopped beside me. I tried hard to flow, to be graceful, to visualise my arms and feet as perfect, keep my dreaded shoulders level and my arms at the right height. She walked in front of me and watched for endless seconds, then nodded and moved on.

Relief spilled through me and my arms dropped. In an instant, her stare flicked back and I lifted them again. This was why I was here – Astrid Ellergren was one of the best, and every second in her class counted, every second took me a tiny bit closer to my dream – the National Ballet School. I lifted my head and checked the mirror, adjusting my chin position slightly. Perfection – a good place to start.

Finally we were sent to the centre in rows, and more practice followed. The back of my leotard was drenched, but I couldn't afford to falter, or show how much I was struggling. Centre practice was about balance – no barre to help – and a couple of times I teetered, then pulled myself up again. Phew!

Just when I thought we were going to spend two whole hours on basic exercises, Ms Ellergren clapped her hands. 'Five minutes' rest, girls.'

Immediately, half the girls fell on the floor; the rest sat. I was glad they were all as tired as me. I sat too and looked around. There were twenty of us, all ages from ten up to about fourteen – only two boys – and everyone seemed to know each other. Four of the girls sat close together in a little group with their backs to everyone, as if the rest of us didn't count.

'They always do that,' said a girl lying on her back next to me. She flexed her legs, one at a time, and groaned. 'They call themselves the Silhouettes.'

'What for?'

'Cause they think they're special.' She grinned at me. 'But they're not.'

'Oh.'

A small, grey-haired woman in black pants and top chatted with Ms Ellergren by the piano.

‘That’s Mimi,’ the girl said. ‘Ms Ellergren prefers piano to recorded music. It means she can stop and start us whenever she wants. Usually when one of us stuffs up. I’m Lucy, by the way.’

‘I’m Brynna. I just started today.’

‘I know. You’re the first new person we’ve had in a year. Most people can’t get into this class and, once they’re in, they only leave when they get too old.’ She peered up at me. ‘How did you get a place?’

I shrugged. I didn’t want to sound like I was showing off. ‘My old teacher knows Ms Ellergren and put my name down, and here I am. I didn’t know this class was so –’

‘Elite? Selective? Oh yeah. And totally competitive too.’ She stretched and yawned, then sat up, brushing herself down. ‘Watch out. If you’re too good, you’ll have plenty of enemies.’

‘I don’t want enemies.’ It was going to be tough enough keeping up in this class. The thought of girls giving me a hard time as well made my head ache. Where was my friend Josie when I needed her? Back in Bendigo, that was where. I’d promised to keep in touch by email or MSN, but we didn’t have a computer at home. Maybe I could go to the library. What would Josie be doing now? Probably heading to the shops to buy an ice-cream, or maybe going to the footy with her dad.

‘Quick – Ms Ellergren hates you being slow.’ Lucy was standing with her hand out to help me up and we got into rows in the middle.

'Girls, we are going to continue now with the short movement from last week. Brynna, you can watch for a few minutes, then I expect you to follow on and pick up the steps as quickly as you can.'

I swallowed. 'Yes, Ms Ellergren.' She was dumping me right in it on Day One! The piano started and I watched pairs of girls dance across the floor in a series of steps and turns, with arm positions as well. After seeing it repeated nine times, I thought I was ready to give it a go. Lucy was the other half of my pair. 'Ready?' she said.

'Ready as I'll ever be.' She set off and I followed, trying to keep her in sight and match her steps. My feet did what they were told, but my arms were all over the place and my face burned as I heard giggles from the other side of the room.

'A good first attempt,' Ms Ellergren called, and someone hissed. 'Come back to this side and do it again. Mimi, please.'

This time, without Lucy to follow, I had to remember it all on my own, but strangely it was easier. Ms Ellergren kept saying, 'Arms up, now out, round them more,' as I danced across the floor. 'And again.'

The third time, I got it right and that earnt me a nod from Ms Ellergren. Whoa! I couldn't believe I'd done it. Lucy whispered, 'Good for you,' and that made me smile, but when I turned around, the Silhouettes were staring at me with stony faces.

For the rest of the class, I stayed at the back, last in

each exercise or movement, careful to pay attention to Ms Ellergren and stay off the Silhouettes' radar. But at the same time, I studied each of them, trying to work them out. I'd had girls in Mrs Calzotti's class who'd been envious of me, especially when I'd won things at the eisteddfod, but they didn't hassle me about it. From the Silhouettes, I'd already picked up big-time hostility, and they didn't even know me!

The leader was a blonde girl called Stephanie; she was tall and slim, with light blue eyes that looked like stainless steel buttons in the light. She wore stud earrings that I was sure were real diamonds and she didn't talk much, but when she did, the others shut up, listened and nodded.

The girl who stuck closest to Stephanie was Ellie; the one with feet like boats, and I felt a bit sorry for her. She was short and stocky, not terribly graceful, but precise. She spent a lot of time whispering to Stephanie behind her hand, but she was also really good at doing it only when Ms Ellergren was focused on someone else.

The other two were Danielle and Penny – Penny was so skinny that her collarbones and shoulderblades stuck out with little points on the end. Danielle was like a dark version of Stephanie, tall and slim with not a hair out of place.

The four of them glaring at me together was a pretty scary sight.

At the end of the class, we curtsied to Ms Ellergren and were allowed to go. As I walked towards the changing room, my knees quivered – from exhaustion, relief or both. But I'd survived my first class without making a complete idiot of myself. I sank down onto the bench with my bag on my lap and closed my eyes.

Pain jabbed through my right ankle. 'Ow!' I opened my eyes.

Stephanie was already past me. She half-turned and sneered, 'That's what you get for sticking your legs out like that, stupid.'

Neither of my legs was in her way, but answering her back would have been a waste of breath. I clamped my mouth shut and rubbed my ankle, wondering how big the bruise would be and whether I could get ice onto it in time. Probably not. I took my ballet shoes off and tucked the ribbons carefully inside. Mum had said it would be a month or more before she could afford new shoes, so these would have to last me.

I sighed, stood up and pulled my jeans and T-shirt on over my ballet gear.

'How do you like Ms Ellergren's style of teaching?' Lucy asked, pausing next to me. She untied her bun and her brown hair spilt out in long curls.

'She's tough,' I said. 'I'm going to have to work double time just to keep up.'

'You'll be fine,' she said. 'But I can tell you – it's practice at home that makes the difference.'

'I'm used to that.' It was how I'd done so well in Mrs Calzotti's class. One lesson a week wasn't enough, she said, so she'd given me lots of stuff to do at home and sometimes I'd had a class with her on my own.

Lucy pulled on her bright pink jacket. 'My dad laid a floor down in our garage just for me. I'm going to get into the special audition training class if it kills me.'

My head jerked up. 'What's that?' I'd read all the information about Ms Ellergren's school, but there'd been nothing about a special class.

'It's the six-week intensive that starts next week. It's for students auditioning for the National Ballet School, but she's only letting a few of us into it.' She glanced at me. 'You're pretty new, so I guess you're not up to that yet.'

'Mmm.' My brain whirled. Why hadn't Mum told me about this? The NBS audition was my whole reason for being here. How could I not be in the class? Did it mean I wouldn't be able to audition this year? Ms Ellergren hadn't seemed too keen on the idea. My skin felt cold and clammy. 'So, what do you have to do?'

She shrugged. 'Dancing and stuff. See you next Saturday.' She gave me a little wave and left.

The room was nearly empty, but I sat, thinking, folding my ribbons over and over. A special class like that would make a huge difference to my chances, but Mum hadn't said a word.

What was going on?

CHAPTER 2

When I went outside to wait for Mum, the last of the mothers weren't bothering to park, just picking up their kids and taking off. Everyone seemed in such a hurry.

A few minutes later, our car chugged down the street and Mum pulled over, tooting the horn. I cringed, jumping into the car and slamming the door behind me. 'I was standing right there! Did you have to let the whole world know?'

'You looked like you needed cheering up.' The car lurched as she took off, gunning it to the corner and out onto the main road. I grabbed at my seatbelt.

'Was your class really awful?'

'No! Well, it was hard. But that's good. I've got a lot of catching up to do, that's all.'

'I thought Mrs Calzotti was a good teacher.'

'She was. But Ms Ellergren is the best. And she expects the best,' I said. 'Did you know there's going to be a special class to train for the NBS audition?'

Mum said nothing and I glanced at her. Her face was pink. 'You did know!'

'Yes, I think it was mentioned in the information.'

Which meant she knew everything and hadn't told me. 'I need that class! Why didn't you tell me?'

'It's a bit soon, Brynnie. It's probably not necessary.'

Suddenly, I could see the dollar signs flashing above her head. 'You mean we can't afford another class.'

'No.' Her hands gripped the steering wheel harder. 'I'm sorry.'

'I'll get a job, then. Delivering newspapers or something.'

'You're too young.'

'I'm not,' I said, folding my arms. 'There're lots of jobs I could do. I just have to look around.'

'You don't need that class!' she snapped. 'All you need is the determination and the passion. You know you've got the talent. Mrs Calzotti told you that before we came down here.'

She hit the brakes hard at the corner of our street and muttered under her breath. Mum didn't often get mad with me, but she was now and I wasn't sure why. She was always quoting those two words at me – 'determination' and 'passion' – like they were a magic spell. If they were, how come they'd never worked for her? Dad told me once that she'd nearly made it into the women's basketball team for the 1988 Olympics. Nearly. I often wondered what had happened.

As we pulled into our driveway, there was a loud bang and a grinding noise. 'Oh god, what was that?' Mum backed up, wrenched her door open and leapt out. 'Tam!'

she bellowed. 'Get out here now!' That was her five-seconds-or-else voice.

Tam came running. 'Mum! Look what you've done!'

Tam's bike lay in front of the car, its wheel bent upwards and the seat half off. Mum's face turned a darker shade of red. 'How many times have I told you to put your bike in the garage? It serves you right.'

'How am I going to get to school without it? We'll have to get it fixed,' he whined.

'*You'll* have to get it fixed,' Mum said. 'I've got no money to pay for it, and it was your own fault.'

Tam glared at me. 'We've only got no money because of *her*.'

'That's enough,' Mum snapped. 'Even if I could afford it, I'd still make you pay for it.'

'Where am I supposed to get the money from?' he said.

'Get a job!' Mum stalked inside and he yanked his bike up.

'It's all your fault,' he said to me. 'There's not even anywhere decent to ride my bike around this dump.' He threw the bike into the back of the garage and stormed inside. I went to check out the bike and the wheel was totally mangled – he'd have to buy a new one. I ran my fingers over the huge scratches in the paint. Tam loved this bike. I used to spend hours watching him and his mates doing jumping stunts at the park. Every time one of them fell off, they'd all laugh like maniacs and get straight back on again. He had no one to ride with here, and now he didn't have a bike either. I sighed, and went into the house.

Lunch was sandwiches and everyone else had already eaten. I munched my peanut-butter-on-wholegrain at the table and drew on my notepad while I thought. How come Tam was told to get a job, but I wasn't allowed? Just because he was older, it didn't mean he'd have a better chance than me. Things were different here in the city. There were tons of jobs I could do – dog walking, babysitting, delivering stuff – I'd find something first and then I'd tell Mum.

In the meantime, I had to find out more about the intensive class and I had a million hours of practice to do if I was going to have any chance of being picked for it.

I needed to work out a training routine. Since we'd moved from Mackles Creek, north of Bendigo, a week ago, I'd had no chance to practise at all – what with packing, unpacking and helping Mum. Back home, I'd been able to sneak into the local scout hall through a back window and dance all I wanted. There was even a rail under the flags I could use as a barre.

But here in Melbourne, my family barely squeezed into this tiny house, and Tam and Orrin having to share a room had caused major explosions. I tried to point out that I was squashed into the sunroom at the back, which would be sauna-hot in the summer, but Orrin didn't care. He'd had his own room at home since he was twelve, and having to share with Tam again when he was sixteen sucked.

I would have offered Orrin the sunroom, but Tam

was the stinkiest boy I'd ever met. His socks would drive a hibernating grizzly bear out of its cave, let alone a smaller sister. How was it possible for a fifteen year-old to smell so bad?

I listed the main barre and centre exercises from the morning class and added others from Mrs Calzotti's routines. The list kept growing, but all the exercises were essential. Where could I practise? Our rickety garage had a concrete floor and every room in the house was carpeted. Maybe if I searched around the neighbourhood, I might find something like the old scout hall.

'Mum, I'm going for a walk.'

'No, you're not.' She emerged from the poky laundry off the kitchen. 'You can help me hang out this washing, then tidy up the lounge room.'

'But –'

'No "but"s. We can't move in this house as it is. If I let things build up anywhere, we won't be able to get in the front door.'

She gave me her look that said, *We're doing this for you, so you'd better do your share and more to make it easier.*

When I'd finished doing jobs for Mum, I escaped and walked slowly around the block, checking out the suburb. The houses were a mix of old and new, but the one we were renting was ancient. It stank of about a hundred years of boiled cabbage and old lady's talcum powder. Some houses were being renovated and one had been pulled down. All that was left of it was a long stretch of dirt with a small pile of rocks to one side.

I turned the corner and there was my new school. I stood by the high wire fence, wondering what it was going to be like. There were only a few weeks left of this term, and that was bad enough, but also I'd be at a new school with kids who had been friends since Prep. My fingers curled around the wire and I bit my lip. I'd never been in a new school with no friends.

It looked like any school, with long, low classroom buildings, a sports field and a hall. On one side was an adventure playground for the little kids, with sails over it for the sun, and in between the buildings was a big asphalt area, probably where the netball court would be.

I walked along a bit further and found an open gate. Maybe it wasn't a good idea to wander around the school on the weekend, but the place was deserted. I wanted to see what the classrooms were like, whether they seemed friendly or not. That was what I told myself – but really I was looking for dancing space.

Through the first row of windows, I could see walls covered in pictures and posters; mobiles and coloured cellophane balls hung from the ceiling. Just like my old school. My eyes filled with tears. On Monday, my friends would all be crowding into our classroom, laughing and shoving and Ms Green would yell at them to sit down and be quiet, like always. Would they miss me? Would they even notice I wasn't there?

What was I doing here? Tam had said I'd ruined everyone's life just so I could be a ballet dancer, and he looked at me sometimes like he wished I was dead. What if I let them all down? What if I wasn't good enough? My stomach churned with doubts. Mum chanting 'determination' and 'passion' didn't help the fear that sometimes choked me – that was choking me now. I swallowed hard, past the huge lump in my throat, sank down onto a wooden bench and wrapped my arms around my body. Maybe it wasn't too late. Maybe we could pack up and go home again, back to live in Nan's house among the gum trees, two doors down from my best friend. Back to our normal life.

No. Mum and Dad had new jobs and we'd moved all our stuff. It *was* too late. We were here and that was that. I had to grin and bear it, as Dad said. A picture of Ms Ellergren popped into my head – not as she was this morning, inspecting our every move and frowning at mistakes, but the large colour photo of her by the studio entrance. The ballet was *Swan Lake*, I was sure, and she was posing spotlit, arms lifted, in a perfect arabesque. Her tutu was white, with feathers and sequins that sparkled like raindrops, and her headdress was made of white feathers too. Everything about her was graceful and elegant and that was what I wanted more than anything in the world: to be in a respected company, dancing ballets like *Swan Lake* with the hope that one day I might be the principal dancer.

I used to dream about it regularly, a dream in which I wore a white tutu and pirouetted across the stage. I'd wake in the morning, feeling happy, and spend half the day there in my head. Suddenly I realised that I hadn't had that dream for ages. What'd happened?

Moving house, my grumpy family, trying to settle in, worrying whether I'd be any good or not – all of that had happened and squashed the dream out of my head. Well, never again. Imagining myself as a ballerina had always inspired me to believe it was possible, and I was determined not to let that go.

I jumped up from the bench and walked past the classrooms to the hall, where I peered through the front windows. It wasn't very big, but it did have a wooden floor covered in gym mats, with piles of chairs against one wall. The door was locked, but there were side windows with catches – maybe I could unlatch a window and sneak in.

'Hey! What are you doing?'

CHAPTER 3

I jumped and banged my head on the window frame. I turned slowly, expecting to see a policeman, but in front of me was a tall, skinny boy with olive skin and huge brown eyes. His clothes hung off him and he carried a basketball under his arm. For a moment, I couldn't speak.

'I'm, ah, just, you know . . .'

'You go to this school?'

'No. Well, not yet. I start on Monday.'

He nodded. 'Mm-hmm.'

'Do you?'

'Last year I did. Now I go to the high school – over there.' He pointed vaguely over his shoulder. 'You weren't thinking of breaking in, were you?'

'No!' But my face grew hot.

He bounced the ball a few times and dribbled it round in a circle, keeping low. He moved so gracefully, I couldn't help asking, 'Do you dance?'

'Why do you want to know?' He held the ball against his chest and stared at me.

'Because I do. Dance, I mean. And you looked, you know, like you did, too.'

He laughed softly. 'I dance with my ball. We're partners. We never step on each other's feet.'

'Do you live round here?'

'Why?' His suspicious face was back.

'Curious – that's all. I've only just moved here.'

'Where did you come from?'

'Bendigo.' I pulled a face. 'It's a big town, but we lived outside it, in the country, in my nan's old house.'

'Uh huh.' He bounced the ball again. 'You want to shoot some hoops?'

'Against you? You're way taller than me. It's not fair.'

He grinned. 'I give shorties a five-point start.'

'Okay, you're on.' I didn't tell him that I played against my two older brothers all the time and had learnt some pretty sneaky moves. We walked past the classrooms to the asphalt court, where one lone hoop hung crookedly from a backboard and the lines on the black surface were so faded I could hardly tell where they started and ended.

'Not really an NBA court,' he said.

'As long as the hoop's the right height. Do I get the ball first?'

He sighed. 'I suppose so.'

'Hey, I don't even know your name.'

'Ricky. What about you?'

'Brynna. Now, prepare to lose.' I bounced the ball and spun round, dribbling it past him and up to the hoop. The ball teetered on the rim – and fell in. One to me! I skipped back, grinning.

'Prepare to suffer,' he said, taking the ball and moving around me so fast I didn't even have time to get my hand out. The ball bounced off the backboard and went in.

'Hmm, six-one,' I said.

Six was all I was going to get. Ten minutes later, he'd won fifteen-six.

'Hey, you're really good,' I said. 'Are you going to be a professional player one day?'

'You've got to be kidding.' He checked his watch. 'I'd better go. I've got to meet my brother.'

'Well, maybe I'll see you around sometime.'

'Maybe.' His brown eyes flashed. 'Or I'll see you at high school.'

'If I last here that long.'

'Me, too.'

Before I could ask him what he meant, he waved and loped away with the ball tucked under his arm. The winter sun cast long, chilly shadows across the court and I shivered. Time to go home.

As I shut the front door of our poky old house, Mum yelled, 'Is that you, Brynna? I need you to help with the vegetables.'

Wasn't anyone else home? Through the window, I could see Tam outside with Dad, talking. Tam was scowling – it seemed like years since I'd seen him smile. 'How come he doesn't have to help?'

'He's busy.' Mum handed me a peeler. 'Do those spuds, will you, and some carrots?'

Peeling. I hated it. My brothers ate enough potatoes to fill a truck and, on the rare occasions we bought fish and chips for tea, we had to buy ten dollars worth of chips to fill them up! I scraped, rinsed and peeled as fast as I could.

'What's Tam talking to Dad about?' I said.

'Never you mind.'

That meant Tam was in trouble, probably for his bike. I wasn't going to feel guilty about that – he did it back home, too, and Dad was always threatening to take the bike off him.

The front door slammed and Orrin staggered into the lounge room. He collapsed on the floor, puffing like a steam train. After a few minutes, he came into the kitchen and opened the fridge door. 'Who drank all the Coke?' he demanded.

'You did, this morning,' Mum said. 'And you should be drinking water after a training run, anyway. Hop in the shower – dinner'll be ready soon.'

Orrin shook sweat onto me as he headed for the bathroom. I jerked back, yelling, 'Gross!' and Mum laughed. I said, 'I thought it was too late for him to try out for the local footy team.'

'Your dad found someone to put in a good word for him. He's allowed to go to training, but he won't get a game unless he can prove himself.'

'He was Best and Fairest for the Redbacks last season.'

'Doesn't count for much down here. He'll have to

start from scratch.' Mum stirred a large pot of mince on the stove. 'It'll be good for him, though. He needs something to focus on – and that isn't going to be schoolwork.'

Half an hour later, we were all sitting round the table, eating and talking over each other. I was telling Dad about my dance class and Orrin was telling Mum about the local footy team and how he'd been talking to the coach. Tam sat in silence, shovelling food down his throat, his eyes on the plate. It was like there was a little black thundercloud hovering over his head and everyone was doing their best to ignore it.

'There's going to be a special intensive class,' I said to Dad, 'but I won't be able to do it.'

'Why not?' Dad asked.

I glanced at Mum and she frowned. 'You've got enough to worry about without taking on an extra class already.'

My grip on my fork tightened and I thought about backing down, but instead I sat up straight, ready to fight. Too bad if Mum was mad at me again. 'I came here to improve as much as I could and have the best chance at the audition. If Ms Ellergren's running a special class, shouldn't we consider it?'

'And what do you think another class will cost?' Mum said, clanking her knife on her plate.

'More money than we've got,' Tam piped up.

Dad's glare silenced him. 'How much is this extra class?' he said.

‘I don’t know.’ I held my breath. Dad was strict, but he was also practical.

‘I haven’t asked,’ Mum said. ‘What’s the point? We can’t afford it. We’ll be doing well to buy her new shoes, let alone anything else.’

‘Let’s find out before we make any decisions.’ Dad piled more potatoes onto his plate. ‘No sense saying yes or no when you don’t know what it’s all about, is there?’

Mum just shoved her chair back, grating it across the lino, and stood up. ‘Orrin, you’re on dishes tonight.’

‘Righto.’

I didn’t dare raise anything more to do with dancing, even though I wanted to ask Dad where I could practise. After the table was cleared, I went out to the garage and scuffed my runners along the concrete floor. Definitely no good for ballet. But I’d seen a shed in the backyard that had all kinds of junk in it, including some rolls of old lino. Those were worth checking out.

I could hardly get the shed door open: it hung from one hinge and everything inside was coated in thick dust. I shuddered as I pulled the rolls out and folded back their edges until I found one that had a smoother finish; I dragged it out onto the lawn and unrolled it. It wasn’t as big as I’d hoped – only about three metres square – but big enough for barre and centre practice.

Dad had put his feet up in front of the telly and I hated to disturb him, but he was the only one I could really ask for help. Mum was in their bedroom, rubbing liniment on her leg. It often ached at nights, but if we asked her how bad it was, she'd brush us off.

I leant against the lounge-room doorway, pretending to watch the news and shifting from foot to foot.

Dad sighed. 'Yes, Brynnie, what is it?' When I asked him to help, he heaved himself off the couch and followed me outside. 'What's the lino for? Was it in the shed?'

'Yes. Is it okay to use it? I know the stuff in there doesn't really belong to us.'

'I'm sure the old girl who used to live here wouldn't mind, if she knew about it. Which she doesn't, because she's dead.'

'Oh. When did she die?'

'Dunno. We got the rent cheap because her family couldn't be bothered cleaning the place up.' He rubbed his face. 'So where were you planning to put this? There's no room in the house.'

'I thought maybe the garage – if you could move the car back a bit.'

'Hmph. Tam's already been in strife for leaving his bike in there. What'll he think if I let you put this down?'

'But this isn't a bike; it's flat. Anyway, I'll lift it up each time I've finished and put it in the shed again. I promise.'

Dad eventually agreed and moved the car back, then helped me brush the lino off before laying it down. 'You'll need a brick on each corner to hold it flat. It's still got a curl in it.'

I couldn't wait to get started, even though it was

nearly dark. I borrowed a chair from the kitchen, put on my ballet shoes and launched into barre exercises. The small square of lino wasn't perfect, but it was better than concrete, even for centre practice. But once I'd done twenty minutes of each, I had to stop. There was no room for anything else, not even a small jeté. I sagged, disappointed and frustrated, wanting to throw the lino in the rubbish.

Mum's shadow moved across the kitchen window blind and she called to Dad, 'What on earth is Brynna doing out there?'

I lifted my arms in answer, into a slow port de bras. I'm doing what you said, Mum! I'm being determined, no matter how hard it is.

The school hall. I stopped, arms rounded above my head. Fifth position, en couronne.

On Monday, I needed to see if I could get that window open and sneak in after hours. Otherwise I was going to get further and further behind in dance class. And how was I going to find out more about the special class? I was itching to ring Ms Ellergren, but I knew I wouldn't be allowed. I'd have to wait.

CHAPTER 4

Sunday dragged. Orrin went to the footy with Dad, Tam was glued to his PlayStation all day, Mum cleaned and cleaned endlessly. She let me catch the bus to the big shopping centre and I wandered round for a few hours. It was boring with no money to spend, but better than helping her with housework. Dinner on Sunday night was quiet, with everyone thinking about Monday – new jobs, new schools. Even Dad muttered with a frown, 'I just hope my old work boots will pass muster at this place.'

Monday morning, I pulled on my new school uniform and stuck my tongue out at the mirror. Black trackpants, yellow top and black and yellow jacket. I felt like a bumblebee, but as I got closer to the school, I started to blend in with all the other bees. Mum said I had to go to the office first to find out where my class was, so I arrived early, hoping the office person would say, 'Room 2463 – that way', but she didn't. She insisted on escorting me personally. I tried to hide behind her – she was a huge woman in a purple dress with bleached blonde hair – but she placed a hand on my shoulder and nudged me on ahead. It was like walking through the school with a neon sign shouting, *New kid! New kid!*

When we got to the room my feet stuck to the floor, but she pushed me forward. 'Mrs Nguyen, Brynna is joining your class for the rest of the year.'

Mrs Nguyen was tiny, only a few centimetres taller than me. 'Welcome to our classroom, Brynna.' Her voice was quiet and musical and she showed me where to hang my backpack, then she pointed to a desk. 'Why don't you just sit and listen for today? I imagine there will be many differences between your schools – or maybe there will be almost none?'

Was she asking me questions, or was that just the way she talked? I decided it was just her, so I nodded.

'Very good. You have been living on a farm?'

'It was my nan's house and there wasn't much farm left, really.'

'You have come to Melbourne because of your father's work?'

'No. We came so I could go to a dance school here.'

'Ah! You are a dancer?'

I nodded again.

'We have another student who is a dancer. Maybe you know her.'

'I don't really know anyone just yet.'

'You will soon,' she said. 'The students here are very nice, very friendly.'

The bell rang, not with a shrill alarm like at my old school, but a chiming melody. It sounded nice. Maybe the whole school was like that – friendly, like she said. I sat and waited, fiddling with my pencil case and lining up my exercise books. Then I tucked my hands together in my lap and tried to breathe normally.

In a few minutes, the room was full of noisy kids, chattering and laughing as they found their seats and hung their bags up or chucked them under chairs. Most of the boys stared at me for a second or two, like they weren't that curious. The girls stared longer, and whispered to each other. My fingers were twisted together so tightly that they ached.

Like me, the others all had exercise books and pens out, ready for the first class, but I had no idea what that was. Everyone had the same books with yellow covers, but mine had pictures of ballet dancers, dogs and horses stuck all over them. Maybe Mrs Nguyen had a rule about no pictures and I'd have to buy new exercise books. Mum was going to love that!

'Quiet, everyone.' There was an immediate hush. 'We'll start with your book reports. But first, let us all welcome our new class member, Brynna Davies.'

Everyone turned and stared at me: twenty-three pairs of eyes zeroing in on my face. I didn't know what to do, so I smiled and gave a little wave. That got a nothing response – they all turned back to Mrs Nguyen as if, having checked me out, they'd now dismissed me. Only one girl near the front grinned and waved back, and I recognised her with a shock. It was the girl from ballet class – and I couldn't remember her name! My face burned, and I slid down in my seat.

The class continued with book reports – everyone had to talk for a minute on a book they'd read that week. When it was my turn, Mrs Nguyen said, 'You don't have to contribute, Brynna. You didn't know it was a class assignment.'

'Oh. Right.' My face flamed again and I wished I'd said something – anything. I'd read some books I could talk about, but my brain felt woolly, and maybe the others would think I was a try-hard.

There was plenty of time to catch up. It was only Day One. I had to chill out.

The class was nothing like my old one at Acacia Hill. Here it was a mix of all sorts of kids – Asian, Middle Eastern, Italian, Australian and two girls who looked like they were from Africa. It was going to take a while to remember all their names and pronounce them properly. Maybe the strange sandwiches Mum made me with sprouts and avocado and curried egg wouldn't get me so many funny looks here.

The book reports went on and on, with some kids sounding so vague they probably hadn't read the book. Mrs Nguyen was onto them. A couple of times she asked, 'What is the theme of the book?' or 'Who are the other characters in the story?' and frowned when there was no answer. While they all did their talks, I tried hard to remember that girl's name, and finally got it – Lucy.

At recess, she was waiting for me at the door. I smiled at her, glad that at least one person was going to be friendly and talk to me. I'd been dreading standing around in the playground on my own.

'I wondered if you'd come to our school,' she said. 'Your mum drove past us on the way home on Saturday.'

'That's my mum – the racing-car driver.'

Lucy giggled. 'The students at Ms Ellergren's school come from all over Melbourne. You're the only one who lives around here, though – like me.'

'How long have you been going to Ms Ellergren's?'

'Four years. But I started ballet classes when I was five.' We walked outside into a chilly breeze and zipped up our jackets.

'Where do you come from?' she asked.

That question again. I explained about Bendigo, then said, 'My ballet teacher, Mrs Calzotti, knows Ms Ellergren. I've only been dancing for three years.'

'That's not long.' She frowned. 'Are you some kind of star?'

Her voice had an edge to it and warning prickles ran along my arms. 'Oh no!' I laughed. 'Just been lucky, I guess.'

'Does that mean you're going to be in the special class, too?' Her dark eyes glinted and I backed off even more.

'Mum won't let me,' I said and her shoulders relaxed. I hadn't really lied, but I hadn't answered her question either. All the same, I was desperate for more information. 'Does Ms Ellergren always have this class?'

'No. The Ballet School auditions are only once a year – that's what the class is for. That's why it's special.'

The wind blew harder, whisking papers across the playground, and I shivered. Mum was wrong. Hearing Lucy talk about how long she'd been dancing convinced me even more that I was way behind. I'd have to practise night and day, but I knew the special class would make a huge difference. I had to get into it!

Lucy didn't notice my fidgeting. 'Ms Ellergren won't let just anyone audition for the NBS – she says it's her school's reputation that's at stake. The special class is twice a week after school, as well as our Saturday class.'

'Three altogether! That's a lot.' I could hear Mum's voice in my head. *And a lot of extra money.* Hunching my shoulders, I buried my hands deeper in my pockets.

'Well, that's the minimum if you're serious.' She pulled out an apple and took a huge bite.

'Are you going to try out?' I said.

'What do *you* think? Mum says I'm not ready yet, but I am. And when I asked Ms Ellergren, she said I could if I wanted to.'

Two little kids were fighting over who got to go first on the slide. One pushed the other away and started climbing the ladder. Three classes a week. How much would that cost? On the other hand, it was only for a short time. Surely that would count?

'Why won't your mum let you try out?' Lucy said.

I gazed up at the dark grey clouds, trying to decide how honest to be. What difference did it make? 'She says we can't afford to pay for three classes a week.'

'Oh.' She finished her apple, threw the core at the bin and missed. 'I guess it's not worth you auditioning then.

That's sad.' She didn't sound sad. Maybe she thought she'd got rid of one more competitor. I shook that thought away – it was mean.

She got up to grab the apple core and I followed her over to the bin, then we kept walking, past the playground, round the corner, past the hall. The front doors were open, but I kept my eyes off them. If I couldn't be in the extra classes, it was even more important to have a great practice space. I *had* to find one.

Mrs Calzotti had talked about what it took to dance for the National Ballet: the training and audition to get in, the technique and strength, the burning desire you had to have, the commitment. Some kids went as full-time students in Year 8 and studied school subjects as well as ballet, but many were accepted before then and went part time to after-school classes. The National Ballet was my dream and it kept me practising every day, even when I was tired out from school.

There had to be a way to change Mum's mind about the class! Although getting Dad onside often didn't work. I'd have to think about it some more.

As we walked back past the hall, the open doors were really tempting. I could at least check out what was in there. 'I need to go to the loo,' I said. 'Can I go in the hall?'

'Um, sure, I guess so.' Lucy looked puzzled, but said she'd wait for me.

I scooted inside and went through the doorway into the assembly hall. It was gloomy and one side was full of stacked chairs, but it was definitely big enough. Excitement bubbled up inside me. It'd be perfect! I raced into the girls' bathroom, unlocked the window behind the last toilet in the row of cubicles, flushed and ran out again. Huddled against the wind, Lucy and I kept walking.

'Did you move down to Melbourne just for Ms Ellergren's school?' she said.

'Yes. And my whole family came too.' Again, I held back from mentioning the NBS audition as the real reason. Instead I told her about Tam hating me, and Mum and Dad and the old rundown house we were renting.

'Your family has weird names.'

'Mum says they're traditional family names, from Welsh and Celtic ancestors.'

Ahead of us, two girls sat in the corner out of the wind. One of them held a ball that she bounced between her legs. Lucy pointed. 'There's Jade and Taylor. Jade's school captain – she knows everyone and everything. Hey, Jade,' she said, as we reached them. 'This is Brynna.'

Jade was the one with the ball. She glanced at me and didn't say hello, then focused on Lucy. 'Are you training tonight?'

The other girl waggled her hand at me, nails covered in sparkly green nail polish. 'Hi, I'm Taylor.'

'Hi,' I said.

Lucy shook her head. 'Can't. If I fell over and got hurt, Mum'd kill me. And then I couldn't audition for ballet.'

'Dumb dancing,' Jade said. 'We *need* you on the team.

Come on, *pleeease*. Otherwise we'll be stuck with Kelly and she's hopeless. Can't even catch.'

'I'm sorry, I can't,' Lucy said. 'You know it's super-important to me.'

I wondered what they were talking about. My guess was netball.

'Thursday's the first semifinal,' Taylor said.

'She knows that!' Jade snapped. 'She's just being mean.'

'I'm not.' Lucy scuffed her shoe back and forth, then she turned to me. 'Do you play netball?'

'No – basketball. With my brothers, mostly.'

'That's close.' Lucy sat next to Jade, who was still pouting. 'Brynna could play. She'd be heaps better than Kelly. Come on, you're only playing Ashfield. You'll cream them.'

'Might not. They've got a new coach, I heard. My cousin told me.' She peered up at me. 'Are you any good? Can you catch, at least? Defend? You must be able to defend if you play basketball.'

'Um, yeah, I guess.' I pressed my lips together, hard, and folded my arms. I didn't want to get injured either, but I didn't want to use the same excuse as Lucy. Especially when Lucy thought I wasn't going to try to get in the class. I stared down at my feet, feeling like a bug pinned to a board.

'She can play wing defence,' Taylor said. 'That'd be perfect. She looks pretty tough.' She smiled at me, but I couldn't smile back. I opened my mouth and shut it again. How was I going to get out of this?

'Ashfield is tough, too.' Jade wasn't giving me any free passes. 'Let's see how you go first.' She stood up and walked a few paces away from us, then threw the ball at me, hard. I caught it as it hit me in the stomach.

I sucked in a breath, hands stinging, stomach sore. 'Thanks.'

No apologies from Jade, just a slight sneer on her face. 'Court's this way,' she said and left us to trail in her wake. I swallowed my annoyance and joined her on the lumpy asphalt court. The other end, where I'd played hoops with Ricky, wasn't so bad, but this end was cracked, with holes and bumps.

As I sized up the disaster zone they called a netball court, Jade said, 'You gonna pass that or stand there half asleep?'

My head jerked up and I threw the ball, hard and fast, the same way she'd thrown it at me, and felt a glow of satisfaction at the surprise on her face. *Take that*. She pivoted on one foot, aimed at the goal ring and launched the ball into the air. It hit the side of the ring, teetered there for a moment, then fell backwards. My feet moved before I could think and I caught the ball, bounced it a couple of times, then looped it up and through the ring. Taylor and Lucy clapped; Jade glared at me.

'You're not supposed to bounce the ball in netball, stupid.'

I shrugged. Jade was as snarly as Tam. I didn't need a friend like her and, right then, if that meant Lucy didn't want to be friends with me either, too bad. 'Guess you won't want me on the team then.' I walked off the court just as the bell rang to end recess. Good timing. I could go straight to the classroom. But as I pushed my way through the double swing doors, my shoulders drooped. So much for finding new friends here. I missed Josie so much – her cheery face, sharing her potato chips, laughing together. Tears prickled in my eyes and I scrunched them up tight. *I was not going to cry!*

Instead, I needed to concentrate on ballet practice. And sneaking into the school hall later.

'Hey, Brynna, wait! Slow down.' Lucy ran up and put her arm through mine. 'Don't worry about Jade. She's totally obsessed with the netball team, that's all.'

'Whatever,' I said. 'I didn't want to play anyway.'

'No, don't worry, you're in the team. Wing defence. She wanted you in, really she did. She's just –'

'Rude?' *Up herself? Aggro?*

'Well, yeah.' Lucy giggled. 'We're used to her. Ms Wilson's the coach. She's good. Training's straight after school.'

'But –' I wanted to practise at home and then come to the hall. I didn't want to waste time on stupid netball with stupid Jade.

'It'll be fine. I'm going to come and watch.' Lucy hugged my arm against hers so tightly that she hurt me. I pulled away as gently as I could.

'I don't think I can come today.' When her face fell into a frown, I added quickly, 'Mum expects me straight home after school. She'll freak out and I can't ring her at work. Sorry. I really can't do netball today.' *Or any day*.

Mrs Nguyen was writing something on the board and the bell had long gone, but still Lucy held me back by the doorway.

'Oh. But you'll be okay for Wednesday, won't you? Please? You'll get to know everyone that way and make more friends.'

I didn't want netball friends. I didn't mind the idea of having just Lucy as a friend, but I couldn't figure her out. Was she really helping me? Or was she maybe thinking it wouldn't be such a terrible thing if I was hurt playing netball?

No, that was silly – and mean, too. Lucy didn't have to talk to me and be nice, but she was, even after I'd walked out on Jade. 'I'll have to ask Mum,' I said weakly.

'Great. The team will be so much better with you in it. And Jade's desperate for us to win the inter-school championship this year.'

I rolled my eyes and managed to keep my mouth shut. Just as Mrs Nguyen began ordering us all to sit down and be quiet, Lucy tugged on my arm one more time and whispered, 'You made that goal shooting look so easy – you could be better even than Jade.'

I slid into my seat, hands gripping the sides of my desk so hard my knuckles turned white. That was all I needed – to push Ms Kingpin out of her goal shooter position in the team. I might as well have broken my own legs there and then.

CHAPTER 5

At lunchtime, Mrs Nguyen wanted to talk to me about what I'd been learning at Acacia Hill, and I was glad to have an excuse not to hang around with Lucy and Jade. By the time the last bell rang, I'd got more used to my class and most of the other kids were chatting with me, even though I still couldn't pronounce some of their names. Mrs Nguyen said she didn't think I had anything to catch up on, apart from maths, and she gave me a bit of extra homework.

'Lucky you,' said Lala, the girl who sat next to me. I'd discovered she was from Sudan – which she pointed out on our classroom map.

I was first home, as usual, and after a snack, I put the lino down in the garage and practised for an hour. Pliés, tendus, ports de bras. Warming up, stretching legs, hips and back, hearing the rhythm in my head like a ticking metronome. Centre work, adage, arabesque. My left leg wobbled and I concentrated on holding strong, balancing, feeling the centre of myself pull up tall. Mrs Calzotti talked about a piece of silver string from your toes to the top of your head, and I imagined it getting thicker and stronger as I improved.

Finally I tried some pirouettes, staying in one place on the lino and focusing again on balance. It was hard, so hard. I yearned to accomplish perfect pirouettes, a series of graceful turns across the floor, my eyes in one spot, my balance exact and my body flowing in one continuous movement. Just *one* perfect pirouette would make me happy! But the little square of lino wasn't a good place to try.

Orrin passed me with a grunt, which sounded a bit like a hello, and I heard the TV go on. Then he headed out for a training run and I picked up the lino before Mum was due back in the car. Tam came in and went straight to his room without saying a word.

I'd spent most of the day trying to work out how I could grovel to Mum so that she'd let me try out for the special class, but what it would take was me finding some way to earn money. Babysitting, gardening (I hated weeding, but if that was what it took), dog walking, car washing. Okay, no one in this neighbourhood was going to pay me to walk their dog. And with water restrictions, I wasn't allowed to wash cars. I'd checked out the whole street and most people didn't even have a garden. That left babysitting. Yuck.

The people two doors down had a boy about three, who seemed to spend most of his time playing on their front porch with ice-cream containers. They also had a baby who screamed a lot. A Vietnamese family down the end of the street had three kids, but they also had an old grandma who looked after them. Maybe I could advertise in the milk bar window? But I was going to need Mum's permission.

I checked the time – surely netball training would be over by now? But it was nearly dark and if I sneaked off to the school now without telling Mum, she was going to throw a hissy fit. I fumed and paced from the kitchen to the lounge and back again. Then I peeled a mountain of potatoes and got Mum's coffee mug ready, expecting her to collapse on the sofa and throw her shoes off. Through a friend, she had found a job working in a factory canteen, where she had to be on her feet all day. Her bad leg often ached, especially in the winter, and I hated to think of her being in pain. In Bendigo, she'd had a part-time job answering phones and could sit most of the time.

She came through the back door, her face drawn and pale. 'Potatoes, Brynnie! Thanks. I'll sort dinner out in a minute.' And she disappeared into her bedroom and shut the door. I poked the spoon into the coffee granules in her mug, pushing them around and around. What was she doing in there? Then I heard the shower going and relaxed a bit. I sat and waited, running through the arguments in my head, so I'd be ready when she came back out.

She'd changed into what I called her gypsy clothes and piled her hair on top of her head with jewelled combs. This wasn't a good sign. Mum usually dressed like this when she was trying to cheer herself up.

'Let's get dinner rolling,' she said.

'Mum, I wanted to ask –'

'Later, Brynna. I'm not in the mood right now.'

'Oh. Okay.' I defrosted the sausages she gave me, watching the microwave plate spin them around and around. If I stood on a revolving plate, would that make pirouettes any easier? No, I'd probably spin off into the wall.

As soon as Dad walked in the door, he was put on barbecue duty. The weather had turned nasty at dusk with a cold change and more showers, and the icy wind whistled into the garage, but Dad rigged the barbie up in the corner and soon had sausages sizzling. I shivered as I took a plate of onions out to him – maybe this wasn't a good night to sneak back to school, but I couldn't stop thinking about that empty hall.

Dad finished cooking, Mum served up dinner in record time, then rounded everyone up to eat. Dad and Orrin tucked in, shoving huge forkfuls of food into their mouths; Mum and Tam pushed and poked at their food, but didn't eat much. I watched them all and chewed slowly, wondering when I could safely bring up the subject of finding a job to pay for the class. Not at the table, that was for sure.

Dad scraped up the last of the sauce on his plate with a slice of bread and said, 'How was everyone's day?'

'Long,' Mum said.

'Boring,' Tam said.

Before I could say a word, Orrin leapt in ahead of me. 'I was talking to this guy today and he reckons I can go down to the local footy club tomorrow night with him. They'll be training and I can suss out whether they'll take on a new player.'

'Sounds promising,' said Dad. 'Go for it.' He waved his fork at Tam. 'What about you?'

'Told you – school was stupid.' He poked a sausage so hard it skidded off his plate, onto the table.

'Tam.' Mum glared at him.

'Sorry,' he muttered, picking it up with his fingers.

'Brynna?'

I opened my mouth, but nothing came out. I couldn't say what I wanted to and I didn't feel like explaining the netball problem. 'It was fine,' I mumbled.

But Mum zeroed in on me. 'What did your teacher say about your school books from Acacia Hill?'

'I can use them.' I glanced at Tam, who was now smashing his tomato sauce and potatoes into a pink mess. His mouth was pinched in a hard line as if he was trying to avoid crying. What was the matter with him? He got up without a word, put his plate on the bench and left the kitchen.

Mum looked at Orrin. 'What's going on?'

'Dunno.' He stuffed a piece of sausage into his mouth.

'You go to the same school. Didn't you see him all day? Is he settling in?'

'I don't know, Mum. Honestly. The school's huge and divided up into sections. I didn't even see him when I walked home.' Orrin finished his dinner and grunted when Mum told him he was on dishes, then went off to watch TV for a while.

Mum shook her head. 'Those boys . . .'

'You didn't say how your day went, Dad,' I said.

'Place is a bit of a shambles,' he said. 'I'm glad I'm

outside, even if it's cold. The machines inside are pretty old – and unsafe, too. They're lucky the inspectors haven't been out.' He was at a place that made plastic pipes and tubing and stuff; in Bendigo, he'd worked at a big hardware place, where he'd driven the forklift. He knew all the WorkSafe rules – he'd been the OH&S rep there.

'What about you, Jen?' Dad said.

Mum slumped. 'It's all right, I suppose. The other women are nice; we have a bit of a laugh. So much fried food there – the smell of the cooking oil gets into your skin and up your nose. Disgusting.'

Dad sighed. 'Sounds like we all had first days that weren't wonderful.'

'Except Orrin,' I said. 'If there's footy in his day, he's happy.'

He laughed. 'True.' As Mum tried to stand up, she winced.

'Go and sit down in the lounge,' Dad said. 'Brynna'll clear the table and I'll rub some liniment on your leg.'

'All right,' she said, leaning on the table for a few moments. 'It's the cold weather does it.'

Dad jumped out of his chair and put his arm round her. 'Come on, love, we'll soon sort you out.'

They left me sitting at the table, stabbing peas. I was itching to go to the school, but it was pitch black outside and I was scared of walking there on my own. Back home, I'd never worried about walking to the scout hall any time I wanted, but here it was different. If Tam hadn't wrecked his bike, I could've taken it. But then Mum and Dad'd want to know where I was going and something told me they wouldn't be happy with my plan. I kept stabbing away and sighed loudly. I wasn't hungry anymore. I cleared the table and scraped leftovers into the bin, then went to my room out the back. From my window, I could see Tam sitting, hunched over, on the back step. His whole body spelt misery.

'Tam?' I hovered by the back door, my heart thumping painfully.

'Go away.'

I took a step closer – was that a bloodstain on his T-shirt? 'Are you okay? Do you want to talk?' I knew the answer would be no, but I had to try.

'Why would I want to talk to *you*? Leave me alone.' He jumped up and charged off into the darkness, head down, legs pumping. I stumbled back into the house and shut the door. My eyes were burning and my throat was aching. He was often grumpy, but he'd never spoken to me like that before. And I was almost sure he'd been in a fight. I wasn't sure whether I should tell Mum or Dad. Tam would think I was dobbing. I thought I'd better keep my mouth shut. It might've been paint, or grease. I couldn't decide – I went into the lounge room and sat quietly on one of our stubbly grey armchairs. Dad had finished rubbing Mum's leg and the sharp smell of liniment hung in the air.

'So,' Mum said to me, 'what did you want to talk about?'

I was still thinking about Tam, his hunched shoulders,

the tears in his voice, and it took me a moment to swing my mind back to my own question. 'I really, really want to do that special class, but I know the extra fees are a problem. If you let me babysit around here, put up a notice in the milk bar, I could pay for it myself.'

'No, Brynna, I'm afraid not.'

'But the class is for dancers going to audition for the National Ballet School. It's important!' I hated the whine in my voice, but I couldn't stop it coming out.

She leant over and lifted my chin so she could see my eyes. 'You think this class is the one thing that will ensure you get into the NBS, but we both know it's not the make-or-break element. You'll be auditioning, with or without the special sessions.'

'Isn't that up to Ms Ellergren to decide?' I wasn't going to give up without a fight.

'That's her opinion,' Mum said. 'But your application to audition isn't tied to her school.'

'Can you at least think about it?'

Dad cleared his throat. 'Isn't this expert teacher one of the reasons why we're here?'

Mum sighed. 'I suppose. But I just don't think we can afford it.'

'I'll give up all my pocket money for the next ten years,' I said.

'Let's find out how much it is first, before we decide,' Dad said. 'But if the final answer is no, I don't want to hear any more about it.'

'Yes, Dad,' I said, and had to be satisfied with that. It didn't solve my problem with Tam, though, but I knew he'd hate me even more if I busted him. I just couldn't figure out what to do, except wait and see.

As I was racing out the door to school the next morning, I remembered that I hadn't asked Mum about the netball team. I'd been going to ask her to write me a note to say I wasn't allowed to play, even if it sounded pathetic. It was too late now – she'd gone to work. Maybe Jade and Taylor and Lucy would've forgotten. No such luck. Before class started, they all stopped me in the corridor.

'How come you didn't turn up to training yesterday?' Jade said.

I was surrounded by them, all waiting on my answer. 'Um . . . I had to go straight home.'

'Do you think you're too good for our team?' Jade demanded.

'No, of course not!' I'd been edging away from Jade and now my back was to the wall. This didn't seem to be about netball anymore and my throat closed over, as if Jade's scrawny hand was gripping it tightly. 'I . . . um . . .'

'Our school's famous for our netball team. We *have* to win the trophy this year. Understand?'

I nodded so hard my neck cracked.

'So you'd better decide whether you're *in* or *out*.'

This time the message was totally clear. She meant *in* or *out* in the whole school. If I didn't play, everyone would treat me like I had a disease, even Lucy.

Before I could force out a reply, even just 'Okay', Jade and Taylor walked away, leaving me with Lucy, who looked at me like I was already infectious.

Great. As Dad would say, I was stuck between the devil and the deep blue sea. For the first time, I understood what he meant.

Lucy pursed her lips. 'You *are* going to play, aren't you? Jade is, like, totally serious. And she's mad at you. She told Ms Wilson that she'd found a great new player and then when you didn't turn up, she looked stupid. She was not happy.'

'But I told you I couldn't go last night,' I said. 'Why didn't you pass the message on?'

'Oh, I didn't stay to watch netball training,' she said, flicking her hair back. 'I was too busy with my ballet.'

The bell rang and there was no more time to talk. As I trudged into Mrs Nguyen's room, I wondered why everything had to be so complicated. I longed for the familiar faces at my school in Bendigo, my friend Josie and my other mates, and all the fun I used to have with them. Tears filled my eyes and I sat at my desk, head down, wishing I was anywhere but here.

CHAPTER 6

While everyone else did silent reading, Mrs Nguyen called me up to her desk.

'I wanted to tell you,' she whispered, 'that next week we're starting a unit on the oceans. I'm afraid you'll be repeating the material from your old school, but we do go to the beach for an afternoon, which I don't think you have done.'

'No beaches in Bendigo,' I said.

She smiled. 'But there are gold mines, and when we do some Australian history in Term Three, you will be able to tell everyone about the gold mine in Bendigo.'

That was *not* something to look forward to. But I used Mrs Nguyen's quiet conversation as an excuse and told Lucy I had to do extra work in the library at lunchtime, which meant I avoided having to talk to Jade again. It was a lie, but I couldn't face her stony face and snappy voice again.

I checked the hall window as I left school at three o'clock and I was pretty sure it was still unlocked. I wouldn't wait for later – I'd come back at four-thirty, when everyone was gone. I raced home, ate an orange and some crackers, packed my gear and headed back to school. There was still one car in the car park, but, as I waited behind a tree by the gate, it drove off and there wasn't a sound.

My heart thumped and bumped in my chest. No one had minded me using the scout hall back home. Here, if I was caught, I'd be in big trouble. I was trespassing. Was it worth it? I thought of the wooden floor and all that space. Yes, it was worth it.

The window was still unlocked, but stiff, and it took me several minutes and a broken fingernail to get it open wide enough to crawl through. My feet scrabbled up the wall as I hauled myself through, headfirst, and grabbed the side of the cubicle to help me the rest of the way, hauling my backpack after me. There! I was in. The palm of my hand stung where I'd scraped it and my heart boomed in my ears, but I pulled the window closed and waited a couple of long minutes to make sure no one had seen me and was coming to check.

The hall was darker than I expected, but at least the gym mats and chairs were still all stacked to one side. I changed into my ballet shoes, tied the ribbons and warmed up before fetching a chair to be my barre. It wasn't easy doing the exercises without a mirror to check that my arms and legs were correct, but I'd spent a lot of time back home in front of the mirror until I was sure I could do it on my own. I'd even had photos on the wall next to me for comparison.

The rhythm of the battement frappé soothed me and I focused completely, moving on to the leg movements that worked my hips and strengthened everything from tummy to toe. In the centre, it was so tempting to start pirouettes and jumps, but I stuck to my routine and felt my arms and legs stretch and ache.

By the time I got to pirouettes, the hall was so dark I could hardly see the mats on the floor, so I stayed near the glass doors at the front. The warm-up was vital because, to be honest, I sucked at pirouettes. I could do one or two okay, but then something went wrong and my eyes would swing away and I'd get off balance. This was why I had to keep sneaking into the hall – I had to have the extra floor room to get them right. What if the audition involved pirouettes? Balance was so important.

I had to work harder and harder, had to be able to pirouette all the way across the hall without overbalancing. Sweat soaked my T-shirt and I alternated the pirouettes with small jumps, but after half an hour, I still couldn't do more than three without teetering and toppling. I stood in the centre, breathing hard, eyes closed, visualising a perfect sequence of pirouettes. Why couldn't I do it? I wanted to scream. My eyes popped open. The hall was pitch dark. What was the time?

Six o'clock! Mum and Dad would be searching the streets for me. I had to run. I caught my T-shirt on the window lock and heard a ripping noise as I dropped to the ground. With the window shut, I bolted from the school grounds, praying that maybe they were late home from work and hadn't noticed I wasn't there. By the time I reached our street, my chest burned and I was sucking in great gasping breaths. *Please, let them be late home, please let them not notice me missing.*

It wasn't going to happen. All the lights in our house were blazing and Dad stood on the front steps with a torch, about to come looking for me.

'Where the hell have you been?' he exploded when he caught sight of me.

'I'm sorry, Dad, really, I was at school.'

'Doing what? School finishes at three.'

'I was dancing in the hall.'

'Why didn't the teacher let us know?'

'Because . . . I was on my own, you know, like I used to be at the scout hall.'

'Brynna –' He took a deep breath and put the torch down on the railing. 'This is not the country, for god's sake. We don't know this neighbourhood and it's not the same as back home. It's dangerous after dark, for anyone, let alone a kid your age.'

'I know,' I said, my voice small, my hands tucked under my arms. 'I just needed to practise, and there's nowhere else.'

Mum rushed out the front door and grabbed me. 'You're safe!' She hugged me, then shook me. 'You had us worried sick.'

'She was in the school hall, on her own,' Dad said. I didn't like his tone.

'What for? Oh, for your ballet.' She let go of me and sat on the front step, head bowed, one hand clutching her hair. 'What a mess. What are we doing?'

'I was only a little bit late!' I cried. 'Nothing happened!'

'It's your brother,' Mum said. She looked up and there were tears in her eyes, tears that made my face go icy cold. 'He got in a fight after school and the other kids gave him a hiding. He won't go to the hospital.'

'Is he okay?' The ice crept down through my arms and legs and I shuddered. What was happening to my family?

Dad's mouth twisted and he looked like he didn't know what to do with his hands. He ended up shoving them deep into his pockets. 'He's got cuts on his face and hands, and bruising.'

Mum sighed, got to her feet and shooed us all back inside to the kitchen. Orrin sat there doing his homework with a cup of coffee. He glanced at me and raised his eyebrows, but I ignored him. I knew what was coming, and dread crawled over me.

'It's time for a family meeting,' Mum said. 'Get Tam out of his room, please, Orrin. I won't take no for an answer.'

After a few muffled shouts, Tam joined us, his face surly and dark. He thumped down in his chair like he'd been asked to turn up for a lynching.

Dad sat at the head of the table, Mum at the foot by the fridge, but as usual Mum was in charge of the meeting. Dad always listened and thought about stuff, and if he decided something, then that was it. Tam and Orrin never thought this was fair, especially if it went against them, but

I'd never worried about it before. I had a horrible feeling that Dad's decision was about to go against me.

Tam slouched in his chair and his face made me feel sick. He had a big lump over one eye, a cut on his mouth that was swelling and purple and another cut on his hand. He'd cleaned off most of the blood and put bandaids on his hand, but they were soaked. He stared down at the table. I tried not to gawk at him, but it was hard – he didn't look anything like the Tam I knew.

'Right,' said Mum, 'we need to talk about a few things. Brynna, I want to know why you were so late.'

I'd already told them! But clearly, Mum expected me to explain again. 'I was in the hall at school, dancing. Doing exercises and pirouettes and jumps. I can't do that stuff here. There's no room and no wooden floor.'

'Who said you could use the hall unsupervised?'

This was what I was really in trouble for. Funny how I'd been so scared of the school finding out. 'Nobody. I sneaked in through a toilet window.'

'Geez, Brynna,' Orrin said.

Tam's mouth twitched.

'That was stupid,' said Mum. 'If anyone had caught you, you would've been expelled. Then what would we do?'

'Go back home.' There was a catch in Tam's voice.

Mum looked at him. 'And what happened to you?'

'Told you. Kids from school bashed me up.'

'Why?'

He snorted. 'Do they need a reason?'

'Yes. What did you do?'

Tam leapt up like a rocket launching. 'Why are you trying to make this my fault? This is where we live, for god's sake! In a city where people knife each other every second day. They don't need a reason.'

'Dad'll go to school with you tomorrow and make them do something about it.'

'What for?' Tam shouted. 'Do you think it'll make the slightest bit of difference? You go in there and complain and next time the knife'll be in my guts – not across my hand.'

'Don't shout, please.'

Tam's face darkened and his eyes glittered. 'You don't need to worry about me. I've already fixed it.'

I'd never heard Tam talk like this before. He'd always been a bit short-tempered, but now he was burning with rage. His hands were clenched as if he was ready to punch one of us. My stomach tightened into a giant knot and I held my breath.

'I hope you're not going to do something silly,' Mum said. She sent Dad a pleading glance – the meeting was getting away from her. He frowned, but didn't say anything; just waited to hear what Tam said.

'I'm going back to Bendigo,' Tam choked out, 'back to my own school. I've already rung Uncle Tony and he said I can stay with them.'

'But –' Mum tried and Tam kept talking.

'There's no use you arguing about it, because that's

what I'm doing. I might not be old enough to leave school yet, but I know where I want to be. I'd rather die than stay here and go to that school again.'

'You shouldn't have asked Tony – you're not his responsibility,' Mum said.

'Well, you weren't going to! You were going to let me rot – all so Miss Ballet Star here could follow her dream.' Tam sneered at me. 'No one else in this family is allowed to have a dream, from what I can see. So I'll work my own out.'

I was speechless, but at last Dad said something. 'What *is* your dream, Tam?'

'To stay alive'd be nice,' he said. 'But I want to be a blacksmith, like Old Teddy Allen. He said if I finished school, he'd take me on as an apprentice.'

'Did he?' Dad raised his eyebrows. 'When did he say that?'

'Before we came down to this stupid place. I would've told you, but it's pretty obvious no one gives a stuff about what I might want.'

'What about you, Orrin?' Dad said. 'What's your dream?'

'Professional football player.' Orrin nodded. 'I'm happy down here because I reckon I'll get a better chance at trying out for the Juniors. I'm going over to the Bulldogs camp next week to talk to someone.'

'Are you?' Dad's eyebrows were about to jump right off his head, but I couldn't even raise a smile. What Tam had said sat in my stomach.

‘I don’t want our family to be split up,’ said Mum.

‘That’s too bad, because I’m going to Uncle Tony’s, no matter what you say.’ Tam charged out of the room and the front door slammed.

Mum tried to stand up, but Dad waved her down. ‘He won’t go far – not after today.’ He sighed. ‘He’s right, Jen. He could’ve been badly injured. If this has happened after only two days at that school, he’s better out of it.’

‘But we can’t afford to pay Tony his board and keep.’

‘We won’t have to,’ Dad said. ‘Tam can earn his own way by working for Tony after school and on weekends. It’ll keep him out of trouble as well. I’ll ring him and sort it out.’

‘Well, I don’t like it,’ Mum said. ‘It’s not right.’

‘Maybe not for us, but for Tam . . . he’s not stupid, you know. He’s thought it through, at least, and knows where he’s going.’ Dad shook his head. ‘Blacksmithing, eh?’

‘So is that it?’ Orrin stood up. ‘I’m going for a run.’ He left and it was just me at the table. I picked at the pattern on the cloth, wishing I could slink down and hide under my chair.

‘Now, Brynna, we need to talk about the hall,’ said Mum.

I opened my mouth, wanting to explain, wanting to tell her I was sorry. Instead, tears flooded my eyes and rolled down my face; before I knew it, I was sobbing, my hands over my mouth. Dad shook his head and escaped, leaving Mum to deal with me. She came around to my chair, knelt down and hugged me gently.

'It's not the end of the world, you know. But you have to promise you won't do it again. It's trespassing and the school won't like it.'

I shook my head. I couldn't speak.

The hall was nothing; it was Tam.

'Here, stop that crying,' she said softly and, when I couldn't, she made me a cup of hot Milo and sat next to me. 'Drink some of this.'

I managed a couple of swallows, which helped a bit and the sobs wound down into hiccuppy breaths. Finally, I whispered, 'Tam hates me. Everyone hates me for making you all move down here.'

'That's not true,' Mum said, but she didn't sound convincing.

'It is. I wish we'd never come. I'll find a class in Bendigo and you and Dad can go back to Nan's place and Orrin can –'

'I don't think Orrin wants to go home, do you?' Mum smoothed my hair back off my face. 'Brynnie, I've seen you dance. You have an incredible talent. If Mrs Calzotti hadn't said so, I still would've seen it in you. Dad and I truly believe we have to give you every possible chance to be a dancer. But there's one stumbling block.'

'Tam?'

'No, Tam will make his own way now. I wish I'd seen it sooner, what he needed, but we can deal with it. The stumbling block is *you*.'

'Me?'

'A dancer's life is impossibly hard. Whatever you're feeling right now is nothing compared to the way it'll be later on. Getting into the Ballet School is only the first of many hurdles.'

'I know that.' I knew she was trying to help, but this was all stuff I'd heard from her before.

'You have to totally believe in yourself, in what you want, what your dream is. You have to pursue that dream, no matter what.' She bit her lip. 'I thought coming down here would strengthen your resolve.'

'Why do you think I sneaked into the school hall? I really wanted to practise properly. That audition's only a few weeks away.'

'I know. And we're doing all we can to get you there, but – you seem to want to be in this special class so everyone'll think you're worth it. But you're the one who needs to feel that worth. That's the bit we can't do for you. Nobody can.'

'You think I don't believe in myself?' Why she was saying all this? Again! Something did stir inside me, though.

'So far, yes.' She sighed. 'But things will get harder, you know – not easier. There'll always be people who are jealous, or who'll try and make you do what they want. You might even find one or two who'll do anything to stop you.'

'How can they stop me getting into the Ballet School? You just said it was up to me, to believe in myself, no matter what.'

'Yes, but –' Her face was drawn, her eyes dark, and she massaged her leg absent-mindedly.

'Is there something you're not telling me?'

She pressed her lips together, shook her head slightly. 'Have you met any nice girls at school yet?'

I stretched my leg out, curved my foot into an arch and avoided her gaze. 'I guess. One girl in my class goes to Ms Ellergren's.' Now was the time to tell her about Jade and the netball problem, but somehow I couldn't. It was as if Tam had created enough drama for one day and I could tell Mum was still feeling hurt and upset about him. So I lied. 'Some of the other girls are friendly, too.'

A smile spread across Mum's face. 'Good. That cheers me up a lot. Let's get dinner started, shall we?'

She levered herself up and went to the fridge; I sat and stared through the doorway at the shapes moving on the TV screen, my mind a million kilometres away.

Mum had been going to tell me something, I was sure of it, but what? Was it about money? About Tam? I shivered, wrapped my arms around myself and edged closer to the heater. Whatever it was, I wasn't going to ask right now. I had to concentrate on ballet and on proving that all this upheaval was worth it. I couldn't let the family down, I couldn't. But Mum was right. It wasn't really about them, even though I felt so guilty somctimes. It had to be my own fight, my own dedication, one hundred per cent. And I was going to make it into the ballet school if it killed me.

But it came back to the same problem – where was I going to practise? If I sneaked into the hall again and got caught, I'd be in major trouble. I'd have to go for a walk and check out the neighbourhood. Then I remembered Tam getting bashed. Maybe Dad was right. I couldn't go out walking whenever I felt like it. But who did Tam fight with? Why? Was I in danger? I followed her to the kitchen.

'Mum, what really happened to Tam? Why would those boys attack him for nothing?'

The way she was stirring the mince was going to make a hole in the pot. 'Tam won't say what happened – he wants to blame everyone else. I think he provoked them, at least a bit. He's angry with us and he paid out on someone else.'

'He attacked them?'

'No, I didn't say that. But he didn't walk away when he could have. Let's leave it, shall we? No use going over it again. We can't change it. Tam will be going back to Tony's and that'll make him happy.'

I set the table for dinner, then headed for my tiny room out the back to unpack my school stuff. My mind buzzed with everything that had happened and I kept seeing Tam's sullen face with the bruises and cuts. Well, he'd got what he wanted, so maybe it was a small price to pay.

I hoped Orrin made it into his footy team and became a big star – then he'd be happy for sure. As for me, I kept hearing Mum's words about needing to believe in myself.

I wished it was something real, like a gold charm, that I could hold onto and feel in my hand, but I knew it wasn't. Despite what Mum said, I was going to try out for that class and give it my total best. Maybe tomorrow I could find another dance space, along with a few flying pigs!

CHAPTER 7

At school the next morning, Lucy and Jade pounced on me just inside the gates. 'Training after school tonight,' Jade said. 'You gonna be there?'

I pulled my backpack off and pretended to adjust a strap, while my brain scrambled to find an answer. I'd pushed aside the netball team again, what with the fuss over Tam and getting into trouble myself.

'I forgot to ask Mum,' I said. 'Sorry.'

'You're kidding.' Jade scowled as she bounced the ball a couple of times. 'What's the matter with you?'

'Nothing. It was just that we –' No way was I telling them about our family problems.

Jade turned her back on me and walked away. Lucy shrugged. 'She reckons you think you're too good for her team,' she said.

'I don't think that. Why's everyone getting in a snit about this?'

'We're not in a snit!' And she marched off to join Jade.

So in two days I'd gone from having at least one friend to being frozen out. No wonder Tam lost his temper. Was everyone round here like this? Josie never treated me like I had a disease.

After silent reading, we had maths and I tried hard to concentrate, but my brain churned round and round, worrying about Jade and Lucy and then zooming in again on the problem of where I could practise. I'd shoved my ballet shoes into my school bag – just in case – and it was as if they were sending me signals. *We want to get out and dance.*

At recess I sat on my own and watched the other kids and knew that lunchtime would be more of the same. Nobody cared that I was lonely and missing my friends at home. Jade and Lucy only cared that I was good at netball, and if I wasn't going to help their team win, I wasn't worth hanging with. After recess, the other kids showed off their projects on sport and I daydreamt about dancing. Then I had a brainwave and, when the bell rang for lunch, I went up to talk to Mrs Nguyen.

'Would I be able to practise my ballet in the school hall at lunchtime?'

She frowned. 'I don't know. If there's no sport on in there, it might be all right. Shall I ask the principal?'

'Yes, please.'

I waited with fingers crossed.

A few minutes later, she came back. 'He says if you eat your lunch and then go to the office person, she'll make sure it's not being used. Have you been dancing for a long time?'

'Three years. There's a special audition coming up and I haven't got anywhere to train.' I didn't tell her I'd already been in the hall.

'Good luck,' she said.

I sat outside on the seats near the office, not wanting to waste a minute. When the second bell rang right above me, I jumped, and then raced in to see the office lady. 'The hall's open,' she said, 'but you'll have to make sure you're very careful in there, or we can't let you use it.'

'I will.'

In the hall, I shut the door, turned on the lights and quickly tied up my ribbons. I only had half an hour, but it was better than nothing. Warm-up first – I didn't dare risk an injury – but then I went from barre and centre exercises straight into pirouettes. One, two, three, head up, eyes on one point. I was getting better, but I wanted to be perfect.

Before I knew it, the bell rang again – and I'd hardly even started! No time to cool down. Off with ballet shoes, on with runners, race back to class. Mrs Nguyen smiled at me as I rushed into the room and sat down, then she started talking about something in the news. My heartbeat slowed down and I listened to her for a few minutes, then my mind swung back to ballet. When I got home, I'd unroll the lino and do another hour at least. Maybe I could find an old mirror in the shed, too, and put that against the wall, or borrow the one from Mum's bedroom.

My ballet shoes were getting too small, fast. Mum had said it'd be another month before we could afford new ones and I hated to think how much pointe shoes cost. Luckily, I stopped daydreaming in time to hear Mrs Nguyen give us some homework on food groups, and after that I tried to concentrate. When the last bell rang, I leapt up, grabbed my backpack and raced out the gate. No way was I going to netball!

At home, I pulled out my shoes again, tied the ribbons and stepped onto the lino. I was so glad none of the girls from class, like the Silhouettes, could see me. For sure, they'd turn up their noses at me dancing in the garage. They probably had huge marble-floored hallways for their dancing, or maybe a dance space in their house. A whole room. How cool would that be?

As well as cleaning the lino and borrowing a mirror from Mum's room – just a small one – I'd pinched Orrin's CD player and speakers. There was so much more to being a great dancer than the steps and routines. You had to feel the music, feel the theatre of ballet, like an actor did on stage. Each ballet told a story, with music and dance, and the dancers had to be inside the music, let it flow through their bodies.

I'd put on extra layers of clothes, but still I shivered in the freezing garage. I did the best I could with the warm-up, then took off my ballet shoes and put on a pair of soft vinyl slippers. They were cheap and it didn't matter if they got scraped on the concrete. From Orrin's CD player, *Swan Lake* began to fill the air and I felt the familiar ripples inside, the notes making me want to float and twirl. I turned it up as loud as possible, then danced slowly on the concrete, not trying to copy the dancers of the real ballet. I was a swan, gliding and turning. If only I was on a polished floor and not concrete – but I wasn't going to let that put me off. I danced, almost feeling the feathery tutu dipping and swaying with me.

'Brynna. Brynna!'

I opened my eyes.

Orrin stood in the doorway, looking grumpy. 'You're supposed to ask before you take my CD player.'

'Sorry. You weren't home. You can have it back now.'

'Doesn't matter,' he said. 'I've got footy training.'

'Again?'

'Made the team, didn't I?' His grin was as wide as a slice of watermelon. 'Tell Mum and Dad I'll be home about seven, all right?'

I gave him the thumbs up and then, as he disappeared down the driveway, I went back to the music, but the feeling was gone. Didn't matter. I had lunchtime at school tomorrow to look forward to, a whole hall to myself.

Just as I was taking Orrin's CD player back to his bedroom, Mum barged in the front door. When I explained what I was doing, she sighed. 'The room looks so bare.'

I glanced around at Orrin's school clothes and shoes and footy jumpers and books, then I realised what she meant. 'Tam's gone already?'

She nodded, her eyes sad.

'But he didn't even say goodbye!' My stomach churned again and I flopped down on Orrin's bed. 'He does hate me.'

'No, he doesn't.' Mum sat next to me and patted my knee. 'He's an unhappy boy right now, but he'll come right. He needs to be where he feels at home.'

'Why doesn't he feel like that with us?'

'Tam's not a city boy, love. He never will be. You can't force someone to be something they're not, just so *your* life'll go better.'

'I feel so bad about him getting hurt. Won't he be lonely up there without us?'

'Maybe. I know I'll miss him – and his cranky moods.' She grinned, then her face darkened again. 'I can't say I'm happy about it, not at all. But I'd rather he were back where he belongs, making his own way, than getting into trouble down here.' She stood up and straightened Tam's bedcovers. 'Now, we'd better get dinner ready. I've got a physio appointment shortly.'

I gaped at her. 'Is it your leg?'

'It's not too bad. But your dad's talked me into having some treatment on it. Someone a mate of his at work recommended.'

This was a first. For years, Mum had pretended her leg was fine and refused to see anyone about it. She'd always said nothing would help. She pulled me up from the bed. 'You're on rice tonight: we're having a quick stir fry. And where's Orrin?'

'He made the team,' I said, 'and he'll be home at seven.'

'Did he now? I'll bet he was happy.'

'Sure was.'

She hustled up dinner and put it on the table just as Dad walked in. He grabbed a beer from the fridge and sat down to eat with us, his eyes crinkling over the top of his can when I told him about Orrin. And when Mum told him about her physio appointment, he laughed out loud.

'All right!' he said. 'Let's get the Great Davies Superstar Show on the road.' Then he stopped smiling. 'Tam get on the bus all right?'

'Yes,' Mum said. 'And he was beaming from ear to ear as well.'

'Good,' was all Dad said.

We cleaned up in the kitchen, while Mum changed her clothes and went off in the car. Dad and I watched the news together. 'How's that lino working out?' he asked.

'Okay. But the school says I can use the hall to practise at lunchtime.'

'Great.'

When Orrin got back he and Dad talked footy, but when Mum limped in, everyone went quiet.

'Has the physio made it worse?' Dad said.

'Not really.' Mum lowered herself into the armchair. 'I've got exercises to do. He said I need to work hard on flexibility and strength.' She waved a hand vaguely in the air, as if she was thinking about something else. 'He said I could play again in a month or so.'

'Play what?' I said.

'Basketball.' Dad was nearly bouncing in his seat. 'That's fantastic.'

'Yeah, I guess so,' Mum said. 'Maybe I'm a bit old for that now.'

'Now, now! You were the one who told me they had a social team at your work,' said Dad.

'Should have kept my big mouth shut.' Mum grinned. 'Orrin, have you had your dinner yet? How did footy training go?'

'Great! Coach says he might give me half a game on Saturday.' His hair was sticking straight up and when he ran his fingers through it, he looked even more like a rooster. 'Where's Tam? I might be able to get him a game in the Under 15s.'

'He's gone to Uncle Tony's,' said Mum.

'What – already? Couldn't he even wait long enough to say goodbye?' Orrin's mouth twisted. 'What a loser.'

'Don't you say that!' Mum snapped.

'Oh, who cares? He got what he wanted, spoilt little toad.'

'He didn't want to be unhappy and getting into fights down here,' said Mum.

'No one forced him to punch that guy, Mum. I've heard other stories about what happened. Tam was looking for an excuse to ditch us.'

'Orrin! He's your brother.'

'You wouldn't think so, the way he was carrying on.'

Finally, Dad stepped in. 'Tam's made his own path and he's got to live with it now. You're right – he should've said goodbye properly, not been in such a hurry to get away from us.' He pointed to the kitchen. 'Go and eat your dinner, son, and then you can tell me more about this coach.'

Orrin headed for the microwave, but his face was sad. I knew how he felt. It was as if Tam had suddenly dumped us, as if he couldn't wait to get away. How long was it going to be before we'd see him again? A lump rose in my throat and I blinked hard. I just had to deal with it. Maybe Dad was right. Tam had gone his own way and we had to focus on what was ahead of us.

Mum sat in her armchair, doing leg lifts, talking to Dad about weights and walking every day. Was she serious about playing basketball again? She'd been really good at it before she married Dad; that's what he told me once. I'd never heard her mention it – in fact, whenever basketball was on TV, she always made sure to change the channel, as if she couldn't stand to even watch it. Now she had a sparkle in her eyes, as if all along she'd been waiting for something to change. What could it have been?

CHAPTER 8

I couldn't wait for lunchtime the next day and if we didn't have to eat lunch in our classrooms first, under the eye of a teacher, I would've skipped the food and gone straight to the hall. When we were finally allowed outside, I grabbed my bag, ready for practice, but the principal stopped me in the doorway.

'I'm sorry, Brynna, but it seems we can't let you use the hall unsupervised. It's an insurance issue.'

'But I'm only dancing.'

'It wouldn't matter if you were just walking around, I'm afraid.'

'What if a teacher was with her?' Mrs Nguyen said.

'Are you offering?' The principal folded his arms.

'Yes, I don't mind. Not every day, but perhaps one or two days a week.' She smiled at me, but my face couldn't smile back. One or two days? For half an hour? It was hardly worth it.

'Thanks, Mrs Nguyen,' I said, 'but I need to practise every day. It's really important.'

'Oh.' She shrugged. 'That's all I can manage. Perhaps other teachers –'

The principal shook his head. 'I couldn't ask, really. And what if other girls wanted to do the same? Our teachers need their lunch break just like everyone else.'

'Don't worry,' I said. 'I'll – whatever.' I was back to square one and tempted to leave a window open and sneak back after school again. But if Mum found out, I'd be in mega-trouble. Wasn't worth it.

I trudged outside and sat down, watching the others play some kind of ball game on the oval that looked like tag, but with weird rules. I'd played tag all the time at my old school – me and Josie were the top team. I swallowed hard, pushing the thought away.

'Want to play?' Lucy asked and I jumped.

'Uh – sure. You'll have to tell me how it works, though.'

She quickly explained and I realised it was what we used to call poison ball at my old school. The ball hit me on the leg and someone yelled, 'You're it, Snail!'

I grabbed the ball and walked with it.

'Gotta bounce – can't do it like that,' yelled Lucy.

I bounced and sidestepped, twirled around and caught a boy behind me, hitting him on the arm. 'You're it.' Before I knew it, I was into the game and having fun, not thinking about the hall or Tam or anything, just running and dodging, laughing and shouting like all the others. It felt great – almost like I belonged.

When I got home after school, Mum was waiting for me. 'No overtime tonight,' she said.

'Is that a good thing, or bad?'

She winced. 'Good for my leg; bad for our money situation. But I have to go and buy a blue top for this social team. Come on, you can come too and help me pick one out.'

Mum couldn't make up her mind, which was totally not like her at all. It only had to be medium blue and plain.

'Buy this one,' I said, holding out a top she'd tried on three times. 'It feels thicker.'

'Are you sure?'

'Yes! Let's go, I'm hungry.' And I wanted to practise before it got too dark and cold. But Dad was getting dinner and by the time we ate and cleaned up, it took every bit of determination I had to spread out the lino and start. The layers of clothing made me feel like an Eskimo ready to go hunting and after fifteen minutes, I gave up. I was freezing and my legs and arms were so stiff they wouldn't do what I wanted them to.

Just then, Mum's boss arrived to pick her up. 'You must be Brynna. Hello. I'm Leticia.'

'Hello.' I pointed to the back door. 'Mum's in there. I'll show you the way.' I could see Mum pulling down the leg of her tracksuit pants – she must've been rubbing liniment on her shin.

'Thanks.' She followed me inside.

Mum's face was shiny and pink and she had a little glimmer in her eyes; as she grabbed her handbag, she fumbled and dropped it on the floor. 'Sorry. I'm a butter-fingers tonight. Hope I'm not like this on the court.' She laughed and sounded like a strangled cat.

'You'll be fine,' Leticia said. 'It's only a little training session and we have a good laugh while we're at it. You'll be taking it easy, won't you?'

'Sure will,' Mum said. 'Let's go, then. See you later, Brynna. Bye, Mike.'

Dad grinned and waved and settled back onto the couch with Orrin to watch the news. I sat with them and worried about my ballet and how badly my practice was going. I *had* to find somewhere warmer and bigger, but where?

'What's the matter?' Dad said, when I'd sighed for about the fifth time.

'Same old, same old,' I said. 'Nowhere to dance. The garage's way too cold at night and I'm worried. Ms Ellergren's a lot harder than Mrs Calzotti. I'm going to have trouble keeping up, let alone improving, if I can't practise properly.'

'Hmmm, I don't know what to suggest.' He scratched his head. 'I called in to the local scout hall on the way home tonight, but they charge rental. The guy said they need the funds and they can't give it away.'

'Did you leave a window open for me?'

'Brynna!' He laughed. 'We're not going there again, all right? We'll find something – it might take a while, though.'

I couldn't wait. I absolutely had to find a space. I was sure Ms Ellergren would tell us on Saturday when the new class was starting and there was a good chance it was going to be that week. Surely Mum couldn't say then that it was impossible!

Orrin went off for a run and by the time I'd finished my homework and was ready for bed, he was back. But Mum still wasn't home.

I read for a while, then heard her come in the front door, followed by lots of laughing and chatter, so I leapt out of bed to see what was going on. Mum sat on the couch, with her leg stretched out over Dad's lap. He was looking at the scar on her shin.

'What's the matter?' I said.

'Nothing.' There was a big smile on her face. 'I've been running around all night like a chook with its head cut off, that's all. And my leg held up way better than I thought.'

I looked at the scar that stood out on her skin like a shiny pink smear. 'So it didn't hurt at all?'

'It did,' she admitted, 'but it was only a bit of an ache. The physio said the more I work on the muscles, the better. And walking will help, too.'

'Oh.' It all seemed a bit weird to me. First Mum pretended like basketball was of no interest to her at all, and now she was right into it again. I didn't get it. 'How come you're doing this now? Why weren't you playing in Bendigo?'

Dad opened his mouth to answer, but Mum held up her hand and he stopped. 'The timing wasn't right, that's all,' she said, but she couldn't quite meet my eyes and a little shiver ran down my spine.

Fine, then, if she wanted to keep some kind of stupid secret. Grown-ups were a real pain sometimes, thinking you were too young to know about stuff. What was the big deal about basketball anyway? I said goodnight and stomped off to bed.

Mum came to the door of my room and I thought she might be going to tell me after all. 'Leticia has promised me overtime tomorrow and Friday, so I think we could buy you some new ballet shoes this week, if you like.'

If I liked! My feet tingled and I jumped out of bed to hug her. 'That'd be fantastic! Can we go on Saturday after class? Please?'

'I guess so. They'll be the cheapest brand, though.'

'I don't care,' I said. 'As long as they fit.' After she left, I lay in bed, imagining how much better I'd dance for Ms Ellergren in shoes that didn't pinch my toes. If only there was a shop where I could buy magic shoes that would make me dance perfectly all the time!

Saturday's class came too slowly for me, but I persisted with the lino in the garage and Mum's dresser mirror, checking my shoulders and arms constantly in case it made that little bit of difference I needed. As we entered the studio, my hands were so sweaty I had to wipe them on my tracksuit pants several times. Ms Ellergren was talking to the piano player and we waited until she was free.

'Now don't be too upset if it doesn't work out,' Mum whispered.

I nodded. I didn't want to think about No.

Finally Ms Ellergren turned to us. 'Hello, Mrs Davies, Brynna. How are you enjoying the class?'

'It's great,' I said.

'We wanted to talk to you – Brynna has heard about the special class,' Mum said. 'I wanted to know a bit more about it.'

'It's open to everyone to try out,' Ms Ellergren said. She focused on me. 'You know my approach to the National Ballet School auditions. Only the best should apply.'

'We put Brynna's application in for the auditions last month,' said Mum.

Ms Ellergren's gaze swung back to Mum, and it had turned icy. 'Brynna still has some technique problems she needs to deal with. There's a lot more work to go yet.'

Steel fingers gripped my stomach. I thought I'd improved! 'I think the special class will help me. I really want to do it.' Next to me, I heard Mum make a huffing sound, but I didn't care. Ms Ellergren was serious. I needed this class so badly that I was ready to grovel at Ms Ellergren's feet.

'How many extra classes will it entail?' said Mum.

'Two extra classes a week until the auditions at the end of July.' Ms Ellergren picked a sheet of paper off the piano and gave it to Mum. 'It's all explained here, including the cost. If Brynna wants to try out, she'll be assessed on her progress so far.'

'That's fine,' I said. 'I understand.'

'Good. Now you'd better get ready for class.' She left us standing there and headed for her little office.

Mum scanned the sheet and shook her head. 'Brynna, I think –'

'Let me at least try out. *Please.*'

'We'll talk about it at home. Now's not a good time. Enjoy your class.' And she left, still looking at the sheet, her lips moving as she added up the costs. All the hope inside me nosedived. If it was going to cost a fortune, there was no way Mum would let me do it.

And if Ms Ellergren thought I wasn't good enough for the class, I had a horrible feeling that I'd be wasting my time with the NBS audition. Mum would say that my application had already gone in, but to know Ms Ellergren had no faith in me – how could I go ahead with that stuck in my brain? The thought of failing filled my legs and arms with lead; I dragged myself into the changing room and stripped off my tracksuit.

'Hey, Brynna, is something wrong?' Lucy stood in front of me, arms folded. She'd been kind of friendly at school all week, but she hadn't made any effort to hang with me. At lunchtimes she'd gone off with Jade and Taylor. I wanted to tell her to go away, but I couldn't be bothered.

'I'm fine,' I said.

We filed into the studio behind the Silhouettes and I noticed Stephanie had on a new leotard with silver edging. All of their ballet shoes looked perfect, from toes to ribbons. But in a few hours, my scuffed old shoes were going to be replaced by beautiful new ones! My feet skipped a little at the thought.

And Ms Ellergren was talking about technique. I could improve, I knew I could. I would work harder, practise more, conquer every step and position. I'd put my heart and soul into my dancing and I'd make it happen. I lined up along the barre, behind Lucy instead of at the end, and felt determination burning inside me again.

Today, the piano kept us in strict time and Ms Ellergren paced up and down, correcting arms and feet by millimetres, nodding and smiling occasionally. She made me nervous – but surely I knew what to do by now? I needed to trust my own body, the way it felt, and then double-check in the mirror, paying special attention to my shoulders and arms.

Ms Ellergren nodded at me several times and only corrected me once! In the centre, it was the same and my confidence grew. The hours I'd spent on the lino were worth it, even if it did take ages to warm up. Now if only I could find a big space and really get to work.

We repeated the movements across the floor from last week, then Ms Ellergren added more steps. She put us into groups of four and spaced us out so we were all dancing at once in our group patterns. It was a bit like square dancing at school and I had to totally concentrate to keep up my part. I guessed everyone else felt the same, judging by all the pained looks.

When the class was over, she clapped her hands. 'Most of you grasped that very well,' she said. 'Next Saturday, after class, I will be assessing those who wish to try out for the special audition class. The dance steps you learnt today will be part of that assessment, so those of you trying out will need to practise them during the week. You are dismissed.'

We made our way out of the studio without talking, because that was the rule, but once everyone was in the changing room, voices rose instantly.

'Why didn't she tell us before?' someone said. 'I'll never remember those steps now.'

'It's not that hard,' someone else sneered. That had to be Stephanie – and it was. Her friends were nodding, agreeing with her and looking down their noses at everyone else.

'Who's going to try out?' a voice asked.

We looked around at each other, but no one said a thing and I guessed they were like me – they didn't want to speak up and have the Silhouettes give them a hard time.

'Well, I heard she's only taking a maximum of six,' Danielle said, 'so two of you had better start working hard right now.'

'What do you mean "two"?' said Lucy.

Danielle shrugged. 'For the two places that are left after the four of us are selected, of course.'

That was so over the top that I couldn't keep quiet. 'Don't count on it. There are lots of dancers here better than some of you.'

'Don't you think you should wipe the cow crap off your shoes before you open your mouth?' Stephanie said.

CHAPTER 9

The changing room went deadly quiet. Stephanie's words hung in the air like a poisoned cloud and the other girls glanced at me and then her, wondering if a fight was about to start. My face burned and I was so mad I could have spat, but yelling back at her wasn't going to help.

'Ms Ellergren would say that everyone has an equal chance,' I said, trying to breathe evenly and not explode with the effort.

'Yeah, so stop being such a bitch,' said Lucy.

Stephanie looked round and saw that most of the girls were nodding. 'Oh, bite me,' she said, grabbing her gear and walking out. The other Silhouettes followed her, leaving smiles and sighs of relief behind them.

'We sure told her,' Lucy said.

I sat and untied my ribbons slowly, feeling the heat leave my face and my heart slow down. I didn't need enemies here, but the Silhouettes seemed to hate everyone and think nobody was as good as they were. It was awful that someone could say nasty things to you and not care about whether they hurt you or not. By the time I got outside, Mum was waiting.

'We'll have to hurry,' she said. 'Orrin's game starts at three.'

'But what about my shoes?'

'We'll go there now. It's only ten minutes away.'

Mum gunned it as usual and we tore along the streets, keeping a lookout for the shop sign. 'There,' I said, pointing at a huge ballet shoe above an awning.

'Dancing Daze, that's it.' She found a parking spot and we hurried inside. The display of ballet shoes drew me at once and I ran my fingers over the pointe shoes – $105! To think that dancers in the Australian Ballet could go through two or three pairs in one performance.

'Brynnie, sit down,' Mum said. 'The lady's going to get you a couple of different sizes.'

Just as I sat on the chair near the display, I heard a familiar voice. 'How about elephant size?'

Stephanie! She was like a bad smell, following me round. A woman in tight blue jeans stood by the cash register with her credit card – probably Stephanie's mother. Her nose in the air, Stephanie came out from behind the big display of sequined ballroom dancing shoes and headpieces in the middle of the shop and added, 'They obviously sell to everyone here, no matter how badly they dance.'

Mum caught on straightaway. 'Your bad manners wouldn't be a sign of jealousy, would they?'

'As if!' Stephanie said and flounced away to her

mother's side, where she whispered something obviously rude. Her mother stared at Mum and me and then turned her back on us.

'Hmph. Lovely people,' Mum said. 'I gather she's in your dance class?'

'Yep.'

'The best schools don't necessarily attract the nicest students.' Mum's mouth tightened. 'I hope she's not hassling you in class.'

'Ms Ellergren wouldn't put up with that.' The problem was afterwards when she kicked me in the ankle! The bruise had developed into a large circle of black and purple that was only just starting to fade. But when the lady came back with some shoes, Stephanie bounced right out of my head. It was lovely to try on brand-new shoes, even though they'd soon be scuffed and worn, and we bought new ribbons too.

There was hardly time for more than a peanut butter sandwich at home before we dressed in our warmest clothes and set off for the football ground. It was near a railway line and every so often a train rumbled past. There were no seats, so we all stood around the railing to watch the game. Orrin didn't come on until after half-time and by then his team was trailing by twenty points. Within four minutes, he'd kicked two goals and Mum and Dad and I were jumping up and down and cheering.

He aided two behinds and then kicked another goal of his own before the whistle went for three-quarter time. 'Surely they're not taking him off,' Dad said.

The other team's coach was on the field, waving his arms at the referee, but then Orrin's coach came out too. 'Looks like the other team's objecting to Orrin playing,' said Dad.

'Is he your boy?' said the man next to us. 'He's damn good.'

'Yes, he's ours.' Dad beamed. 'He's legal to play – got clearance from his old club, so there's nothing they can do.'

'Hope not,' said the man. 'We need a win for a change.'

The whistle blew and the last quarter started, with Orrin still on. He kicked another goal, aided two more and at full-time his team had won by seventeen points. The crowd clapped like mad as they ran off the field. I could tell that Dad was busting to go into the change rooms, like he did at home, but he held back and we bought hot tea and chocolate from the caravan while we waited for Orrin.

He came out about fifteen minutes later and, when he saw us, a huge grin split his face. 'Hey, you guys, I wondered if you'd wait.'

'Well done, son, well done.' Dad slapped him on the back several times.

'Yeah, thanks. The coach is pretty pleased. Says I can play a full game next week.'

'Fantastic,' Dad said. 'Do you want a lift home?'

'Um, no, they're having a bit of a team celebration. I thought I might stay.'

'Righto. No drinking though, okay? You're well under-age.'

'Okay, Dad.' Orrin shrugged, but he didn't look too pleased.

'You're still on probation here, and off-field behaviour's a big deal these days. Last thing you need is a scout from one of the clubs checking you out when you're too drunk to behave yourself.'

Orrin's face reddened and he nodded. Dad had hit home with that one.

'Anyway, give us a call if you want to be picked up,' Mum said, and off we went. After dinner, I sewed ribbons onto my new shoes, saying a wish with each stitch. It was a superstition I couldn't stop following – *one day, Australian Ballet*.

On Sunday, while Dad and Mum stayed in bed with the papers and their breakfast, I went for a walk. If I couldn't find a big space for practising the dance steps Ms Ellergren had given us, I wouldn't have a hope of being picked for the class. Since there was nowhere at home, I had to find one close by.

I hadn't really noticed the rest of our suburb before – I walked to school and once I'd walked to the shopping centre – so I tried to cover the streets in a grid, using school as a central point so I wouldn't get lost. A lot of the houses were old and rundown, with scraggly lawns and wrecks of old cars in the driveways. Some streets had rows of units that all looked the same and in one street there was an old people's home, with half a dozen bent-over oldies sitting out in the garden in wheelchairs.

The third time I ended up back near my school, I

spotted Ricky on the court with his basketball and went in to say hi. He was dressed in an old red ski jacket with a striped Essendon beanie on his head.

'Hey, the dancer,' he said. 'Gimme five.' He whacked my hand and laughed. 'You don't look happy. What's up?'

'Just stuff,' I said.

'Want a game of one-on-one?'

'Are you going to crush me like last time?'

'Little shortie like you, I'll give you a seven-point start.'

'Okay.' I grabbed the ball off him and ran up to the goal, throwing and making a hoop. 'That's eight for me.'

He just laughed, took the ball and ran circles around me. No matter how I tried, I couldn't get the ball off him, and when it was my turn, he whisked it out of my hands every time.

'Fifteen–eight,' he said. 'You're getting better.'

'Yeah, right,' I puffed.

'What you doing out wandering around on a dead old Sunday?'

'Looking for a space for my dancing.'

'What space? Like the school hall?'

'Yes, but I'm not allowed in there, not even in school time now. Hey, do you know anywhere?'

'How big a space you need?'

'Half the size of this court would do.'

He scratched his beanie. 'I might know somewhere, but it gets used a lot, so – no harm in asking, maybe.'

'Where? Can you take me there?'

'Not so fast. It might not be open. It's the youth hall, by the park.'

'Can we look anyway? Please?'

He grinned. 'Take it easy, shortie.'

'It's really important to me.' Was the youth hall a possibility? I jiggled on the spot, my body warm from the one-on-one, my legs already flexing and wanting to dance. 'Can we go now?'

'Okay, okay.' He tucked the ball under his arm and ambled over to the gate. I followed him out of the school grounds and along a wide curving road. 'That's the park, for the football freaks,' he said, pointing to our left, 'and that's the tennis courts for the tennis freaks.'

'So am I the dance freak?' I said.

'Probably.' He did a little sidestep, a jive thing with his feet, and rolled the ball between his hands. 'That brown shack there is the youth hall.'

'Oh.' It was old and shabby. 'What's in there?'

'Just some rooms for meetings and kids' clubs and stuff. There used to be a basketball stadium next to it, but it burnt down last year.'

'How come?'

'Team from over there,' he waved his hand, 'got beat by our team and they came back next night and torched it. Man, what a fire. So now we got nowhere to play.'

'Did the police catch them?'

'No evidence, but we knew it was them.'

'So do you play in the team?'

'Got no team now, with no court.'

'But you're really good. That's not fair, that you can't play.'

'Whatever.' He shrugged it off, but he looked pretty sad.

We were nearly at the front door, which was propped open with a brick. 'It's open. Can we go in and ask?'

'Not me.' He stopped where he was, by the fence. 'I'm banned. This is as far as I go.'

CHAPTER 10

I stared at Ricky. What could he have done that was so bad? Burnt something down? I couldn't ask – it would sound really rude. 'But –'

'Chill.' He shrugged. 'I just got in a fight, that's all. No big deal.'

'Oh.' Voices were coming from inside the hall entrance, but after a few seconds I worked out it was a TV. 'Well, you wait here, all right?'

'Whatever.'

I wasn't sure he actually would, but I couldn't force him. I went in and found myself in a large room with couches, a TV and a small kitchen to one side. Five big teenage boys lounged on the couches, eyes glued to the TV, ignoring me.

'Excuse me.'

No response. No one even turned his head.

'Excuse me,' I shouted.

Five pairs of eyes settled on me. Silence, apart from the gunfire on TV.

'Who's in charge of this place?'

Five heads turned back to the TV, but one hand pointed down a narrow corridor. I edged around the couches and headed for an open door in the distance. It was an office and inside was a man at an untidy desk, writing on a notepad. I knocked and he jumped.

'What? Oh, hello.' He tried a smile. 'Sorry, I thought you were one of the boys.'

'No, I'm Brynna.'

'Yes, well, what can I help you with?'

I explained and as he sighed his weedy moustache twitched. 'No big rooms here, I'm afraid. Except that one out there full of couches. Sorry.'

My heart fell down to my stomach. 'But – a small room might be good. Please? Can we at least look and see?'

'Lots of things on here after school, you know. We have a lot of kids come in; can't give one kid a room of her own. Sorry.'

'Every room is used all the time, every night?'

'Er – not every night. Most nights. I've got a timetable, see?' He pointed at a huge chart on a whiteboard that had quite a few free spaces on it. I went closer.

'What's the PP room?'

'Ping-pong. There are two tables in it.' He mimed hitting a ball with a ping pong bat.

Two tables meant it was a good size. 'It's only used on Tuesdays and Thursdays.'

'Ping pong nights.'

'It's free between four and five-thirty the other nights. Can I have it then?'

'There are two *tables* in it.'

Maybe Ricky was banned because he whacked this man with a ping pong bat, like I wanted to. I took a deep breath. 'If I promised to fold up the tables and put them back again, could I please use the room on Mondays, Wednesdays and Fridays?'

'Well – I suppose that'd be all right.' He held up a marker. 'Want to write yourself into the timetable?'

'Yes, thank you.' I wrote 'Brynna Davies' in neat capital letters, hoping no one would come along and wipe it off. Then I noticed that the man had accidentally given me a permanent marker and I held back a giggle. 'I'll be here on Monday at four,' I said. 'Thank you.'

Outside, Ricky was sitting on a park bench further along, holding his ball against his stomach, with his beanie pulled down low.

'Guess what?' I tapped him on the shoulder and he jumped about ten centimetres.

'Take it easy!' His face was pale. 'I'm busy being incognito.'

'What does that mean?'

'Not being me.'

'Why? Did you think that guy inside was going to come out and have a go at you?'

'Him? Nah. It was them.'

I followed his stare to a police car on the other side

of the park. 'You're not doing anything.'

'Don't need to be doing nothing,' he muttered. 'Come on, let's go to the shops.' As we walked, he said, 'So, did the man inside help you out?'

'He wasn't keen at first. Said the place was really busy and he couldn't fit me in.'

'Yeah, sure it is. Only kids that go there after school are the ones whose parents lock them out of the house till they get home from work.'

'Why would they do that?'

'Stops them wrecking the house and eating all the food.' He elbowed me. 'You really are from another planet, hey?'

At the strip of shops nearby, Ricky bought a drink and we sat on a bench, sharing it and watching cars drive past and the occasional person buy something at the milk bar.

'What year are you in at school?' I asked.

'Year eight, when I go.'

'You're tall,' I said. 'And fast. That's what makes you good at basketball.'

'Doesn't make me good at maths or reading, though.'

Suddenly the police car cruised to a stop in front of us. Ricky froze and I tensed as well; I had the feeling he was about to make a run for it. The policeman driving had his window open. He leant out on a beefy arm covered in thick sandy hair, looked me up and down and then zeroed in on Ricky.

'Riccardo Costa. Nothing better to do?'

'Just talking,' Ricky said defensively.

'I see. Where have you been today?'

'Around here. Park.'

'Sure about that? You weren't in Kmart over by the cinemas?' The policeman's eyes slid across to me again. 'Who's your little friend?'

'No, I wasn't in Kmart and she's not doing anything wrong.'

My skin prickled and I sat up straighter. What was going on? 'I –'

'You don't need to talk to him,' Ricky cut in.

'I'm keeping an eye on the neighbourhood,' the policeman said. 'I like to know who's new. You need to keep better company, young lady.'

Before I could think of an answer that wouldn't get me into trouble, he drove off. As soon as the car was out of sight, Ricky jumped up and threw his bottle against the brick wall behind us. 'I wasn't doing nothing!' he shouted. 'Why can't he leave me alone?'

Then he saw me hunched down on the seat. My heart was pounding so hard I thought I was going to faint.

'Hey, man, I'm sorry.' He grabbed his ball and started walking away from me, then he came back. 'I am really sorry, all right?'

I stared up at the bright tears in his eyes and at his twisted mouth. What could I say? I'd seen that look on Tam's face, the utter frustration at the world and its unfairness, and I suddenly understood why Tam had to leave. But Ricky had nowhere else to go.

'It's fine, truly.' I managed a wobbly smile. 'You're like my brother.'

'Yeah? Well, I'd better run. See you round, hey?'

'Yep.' I watched him jog down the street and around the corner before I set off in the other direction for home. Mum and Dad would probably want to check out the youth hall on Monday before they'd let me practise there, but maybe it was better if they didn't meet Ricky.

CHAPTER 11

Mum wasn't too keen on me using the youth hall, but Dad stuck up for me. 'I'll go down with her and check it out,' he said. 'It's the local youth place – can't be too bad.'

'There's a man who's in charge,' I said. 'You can talk to him.'

We arranged to go at four and Dad said he'd help with the tables, but he couldn't do it all the time. 'I never know when I have to work overtime,' he said.

I thought maybe I could ask Ricky to help, if I could find him again.

At school the next morning, Lucy met me by the gate. 'Mum said I can try out for the class,' she said, jigging about. Her long dark curls blew across her face and she brushed them away. Her cheeks were flushed. 'She's bought me new shoes!'

'Didn't you say last week that you weren't going to try out?'

'Well, yeah, but –' She waved one hand, flicking my question aside. 'I knew she'd say yes in the end.'

'That's great.' I wasn't sure what to say. Mum and Dad hadn't told me I could, but they hadn't said no either.

'Pity *you* can't try out, though,' said Lucy.

'I'm hoping I –'

'Hey, there's Jade. What's wrong with her?' She ran over to join Jade and I followed slowly. Jade's face was dark and scowling and I didn't want to know why.

Lucy's mouth gaped. 'You're kidding! That's terrible!'

'Stupid woman,' Jade said. 'Why did she have to go skiing?'

Lucy turned to me. 'Ms Wilson broke her leg yesterday. She can't coach the netball team anymore.' She swung back to Jade. 'Omigod, what are you going to *do*?'

'We're probably going to lose,' Jade snarled. 'What do you think?'

I wanted to say it was only netball, but I knew that'd cause World War III, so I bit the inside of my cheek to stop the words coming out of my mouth. Taylor came up behind us and we heard the bad news all over again.

'We can do it without Ms Wilson,' Taylor said, but her voice was uncertain.

'Hardly,' said Jade. 'Not when we have to have Kelly in the team.' She threw me a venomous look.

I took a deep breath and said, 'Maybe another teacher can coach you.'

'Ha. As if.' Jade flounced away, dragging Taylor with her, as if staying around me might be contagious. Lucy gazed after them miserably.

'I know she wants me to play,' she said, 'but I just can't.' She paused. 'Why won't you play for them?'

I thought fast. 'Dancing's really important to me, too. Besides, I hate netball.'

'Don't ever say that to Jade. She'd cut your tongue out.'

The bell began to ring and we walked towards our classroom. 'I tried to practise that dance Ms Ellergren gave us,' Lucy said. 'It's hard. I couldn't remember all the steps.' She glanced at me sideways. 'Can you?'

'Yes, I think so.' I'd actually written them down, to make sure I didn't forget a single one.

'Could you – could you go over them with me? Please?'

The first thought that leapt into my head was that if I helped her, she might beat me into the class. Then shame burned through me, right up into my cheeks. I ducked my head. 'Yeah, sure.'

'Oh thanks, you're a star!' Lucy's smile made me feel better. Mum had said over and over that it wasn't about competing with others – you had to excel for yourself, be your own super best. Comparing or being rivals was pointless. Ballet was like anything you wanted to be good at – your biggest opponent was the chorus of little voices inside your own head. You had to answer them back!

Right then, I nearly opened my mouth and told Lucy about the youth hall, but something made me keep it shut. It wasn't that I wanted to be mean and not share, but I needed to work out on my own. I needed to focus and be able to make mistakes and then correct them without someone watching me and offering suggestions. To me, Ms Ellergren was the only one who could truly help.

I couldn't wait for the last bell to ring. All day, Lucy, Jade and Taylor kept talking about the netball team and the semi-final game until I wanted to strangle them. I didn't want to discuss it, so that put me on the outside again. Once, Jade even hooked her arms through Lucy's and Taylor's, pulled them away to talk and left me sitting alone, watching the boys kick the footy around. Josie would never have done that. I scrubbed away the one stupid tear that crept out and concentrated on picturing dance steps in my head as I rehearsed mentally.

Was I supposed to remind Lucy that she'd asked me to give her the sequence of steps? I watched her and Jade, arm in arm. No, she could ask again whenever she was ready.

I ran home after school, pushing Jade and the others out of my mind, changed into my leotard and tights and pulled trackies on over the top. Dad picked me up and we headed for the youth hall. The boys on the couches were gone, and a short, bald man was sweeping the hallway floor.

'Can I help you?' he said.

'My daughter has arranged to use one of your rooms for her dancing.'

'Oh, that can't be right,' said the man. 'No one told me.'

Sheesh! 'The man who was here yesterday wrote me in on the timetable.'

The bald man frowned. 'I'm in charge here and he should've asked me first. We have an open-door policy for everyone, but giving a room just to one person – well, that's not really fair.'

'There's no one else here!' I said.

'Brynna,' Dad warned. 'The room is not used very much apparently, and –'

'Which room?' the man snapped. 'We're always busy.'

I could see yet another dance space disappearing before my eyes. 'Please, can you listen for a moment? It's the ping pong room and the other man told me it's only booked Tuesdays and Thursdays. I promise I only need it for an hour or so and I'll keep it really tidy and put the tables back and everything. It's just –' My voice wobbled and I felt like a wuss, but I couldn't help it. 'There's nowhere else and if I can't practise for this really important audition, then it'll all be for nothing.'

'Now, look, it's not that bad,' Dad said, trying to calm me down.

'It is! It's really, really important to me!' Another one of those stupid tears trickled down my face.

'Oh, well – I suppose I might be able to make a small exception.' The bald man seemed edgy with me crying and there were beads of sweat on his shiny head. 'I'll need to double-check the timetable first.'

'That'd be great,' Dad said.

We waited while the man trundled down the hallway into the office and I could hear him umming and ahing, then he came back. 'Yes, Arthur did book you in, although it doesn't look like his handwriting.'

I was about to admit it was mine, but decided it was better to keep quiet.

'So it's okay then?' Dad said.

'I suppose so. But I'll need to give you a list of rules and regulations and you'll have to ensure the two tables are returned to their correct position.'

'Not a problem,' said Dad.

But when we got to the room and Dad saw the tables, he hesitated. 'Brynna, you won't be able to manage these on your own,' he muttered.

'I've got a friend who can help – don't worry, Dad. I'll work it out. Can you please help me for now? And come back at five-thirty? Please?'

He nodded and we folded the two tables and stacked them against the wall while the bald man watched, not offering to help us.

'Right then,' said Dad.

'You need anything else?' the man asked.

I scuffed the floor and felt grit under my sole. 'Can I borrow your broom and sweep the floor, please?'

'Certainly.' That made him smile. Maybe he was the only one who ever cleaned up around the place. Ten minutes later, the floor was clean and I was on my own. Fantastic! I had no music, but I'd work that out before Wednesday. For now, it was time to warm up, then take off my winter layers and practise in my leotard. And with my new shoes!

With a chair as a barre, I went through all the exercises, letting my feet and legs work on their own, while I focused on my arms. Were my shoulders dropping or hunching? I needed a mirror! Then I moved to the centre and fifteen minutes later I was ready to work on the dance steps Ms Ellergren gave us. It was the one thing I had going for me – a good memory for sequences of steps.

I danced the steps several times to make sure I remembered them in the right order, then slowed down and went through each position, trying to feel where my body was, especially whether my arms and shoulders were correct, and toes turned out. Then I danced the sequence again, this time imagining the piano music and putting more feeling into it.

Finally, I focused on pirouettes. I had a feeling that Ms Ellergren was going to want to see some this week and I needed to get them working better. As usual, I managed two okay, then with the third, I went slightly off-balance and teetered as I came back into fifth position.

I tried again. This time I nearly fell over. I had no excuse – I wasn't feeling dizzy or tired. What was the problem? What was I doing wrong?

I spread my arms out and stood, eyes closed, trying to stay calm, but my heart raced like a grasshopper in a panic. Pirouettes were difficult, sure, but they were part of every dance. I had a suspicion now that the tottering was connected with my arms not being right and that made me panic even more. Ms Ellergren was bound to ask me to do some and I was terrible at them. And what about the NBS audition? This could ruin everything.

How on earth was I going to get them right?

CHAPTER 12

After a few minutes of deep breathing, I calmed down a bit and told myself I could do it. It was a technique – I knew how to do this. I was determined to work it out.

I thought back to my classes with Mrs Calzotti. Some days I'd been doing several things wrong with my pirouettes; most days she'd said it was a matter of confidence, but she'd sometimes mentioned my head position. 'Keep your chin up, eyes on one spot.' The basic rule, really, but I'd start with that, make sure my arms were correctly in first, and see what happened.

The first pirouette was reasonable, the second one tottery. I needed to focus! The third one was good, the fourth as well. The room was only big enough for four. Maybe moving across the floor so much was the problem; I tried to stay in one place.

One, two, three, four, five! I did it! Not one wobble!

I tried again. Again, five in a row, all good. I knew I could get it right if I had the space and the time on my own. Relief flooded through me and I gave myself a little curtsey of celebration.

To finish, I danced Ms Ellergren's steps again, and on the last jeté, I heard clapping.

'Lovely!' Dad was standing in the doorway.

I laughed. 'I finally got those pesky pirouettes working.'

'They're not catching, are they?'

We put the tables back and headed home. The bald man was nowhere in sight, but the five boys were watching TV on the couches again. It was some quiz show and they were all shouting at the contestants. Dad raised his eyebrows, but said nothing until we got into the car.

'Are they there all the time? Unsupervised?'

'I don't think so.'

He shook his head and started the car. 'Better get home. Your mother's got a physio appointment tonight.'

'She's really keen to get back into basketball,' I said. 'It seems a bit weird to me.'

'Why's that?'

'Because before, she acted like she hated it. Now she can't wait to play.'

He cleared his throat. 'She's having a bit of fun, that's all.'

'But if she's so happy about it, how come she never played in Bendigo? There were heaps of social teams up there, and a competition side.'

'It was – hard for her up there, that's all.' His face was pink and he didn't look at me. 'Maybe you should ask her about it.'

I shifted uneasily in my seat. How could I ask Mum

when even Dad, who was wide open about everything, wouldn't explain it to me? A small thing was growing into a mountain and I couldn't work out why.

Straight after dinner, I sat at the kitchen table and did my maths homework, then started reading a book that I had to write a review of before the following week. But my mind kept drifting away from the page and out to Mum watching TV with Dad. A few minutes later, she came in.

'Want a hot chocolate?' she asked, turning the kettle on.

'Yes, please. Where's Orrin?'

'Gone for a run. Dad said the youth hall works well.'

'Yes, it was great.' The silence stretched out as I watched her spoon coffee and chocolate into mugs. It was now or never. I took a breath. 'Mum, why didn't you play basketball in Bendigo? Why now?'

It was her turn to be silent and she kept her back to me for several long moments before turning around. 'Let me make this coffee first.'

I waited, pressing my lips together hard and trying to focus on the blurred pages I was studying. She put my chocolate next to me, sat down and took a few sips of her coffee. 'I haven't played for a long time, Brynna. Because of my leg.'

'I know. Dad said you used to be really good.'

'Hmm, well –' Her mouth quirked up at one corner. 'I was good enough to be picked for the Olympic team in '88. Is that considered *really* good?'

'Olympics?' My jaw dropped. 'Truly?'

She laughed. 'Don't look so amazed.'

'What happened? Did you win a medal?' I gripped the mug and stared at her.

'No, I didn't.' She laid her hands flat on the table, fingers splayed, then clasped them together. Her knuckles were white. 'The team came fourth. They did fantastically well. Better than anyone expected. But I didn't play. That's when I was injured.'

'That's terrible! You must have been devastated.' I wanted to rush around the table and hug her, but I stayed in my chair. She looked like she might push me away.

For a moment, Mum's chin trembled, then she shrugged. 'These things happen. I had my chance and it didn't work out. But life goes on.'

Something wasn't right in the way she was talking. She wasn't telling me everything. 'Did you keep playing after your leg got better? You could have been in the '92 team, right?'

Mum pulled at her hair, then she shook her head and smiled, as if banishing bad thoughts to the dark outside. 'I did my best and I moved on. I coached for a few years and then I had you kids. My life filled up with nappies and cooking and that was plenty for me.' She stood up. 'Time to watch my favourite show. Have you finished your homework?'

'Yes.' I packed my books away and took my school bag out to my room. The air was frosty and I shivered, but the goose bumps on my skin persisted long after I was snug and warm under my doona. Every time I thought about Mum being picked for the Olympics, my breath caught. It was so fantastic and yet she'd never mentioned it before. I understood why she'd given up playing – the disappointment must've been totally awful – but still, giving up just didn't seem like her. There was still something she hadn't told me, something vital, and it was like a fish hook in my brain. I had to find out what it was.

The following day, when I walked through the school gates, the first thing I saw was Jade's scowling face. I hesitated, wanting to veer away and head for my classroom, but Lucy was right behind me. She grabbed my arm and dragged me over to where Jade and Taylor stood by the school sign. 'Hi,' Lucy chirped. 'Did you watch "Dancing with the Stars" last night?'

Jade cut in. 'We were too busy having a team meeting. It's a disaster. Nobody wants to coach us.'

Her eyes glittered with tears and I felt sorry for her, but I knew I'd feel a lot sorrier if she wasn't so aggro about the whole thing.

'Nobody at all?' Lucy said. 'But – does that mean you can't play?'

'Probably,' said Taylor. 'We can't even train on school grounds now without an adult supervising.'

'It's not fair!' Jade said. 'We can win the trophy, I know we can. Even without a coach. But none of the stupid teachers wants to help.'

It sounded a bit weird. 'Can't one of your parents be the supervisor? Won't your mum help?'

Jade glared at me. 'Don't be stupid. She wouldn't know how.'

Before I could stop myself, my mouth opened and the words spilt out. 'Pity my mum only coached basketball. But seeing as how basketball's stupid, too –' I was paying Jade back for the way she'd sneered at my goal shooting, but it was the dumbest thing I could've said and now it was too late to take it back. Jade's eyes lit up, she took a step towards me and grabbed my arm.

'That doesn't matter. The principles are the same. Besides, she only needs to stand on the sidelines.' Her grip on my arm pinched like a crab's claw. 'You *have* to ask her. She's our last hope.'

'She can't. She's injured.' I tried to pull my arm away, but that only made it hurt more.

Jade was on a mission, though. 'Doesn't matter. Like I said, she only has to stand there and blow a whistle.'

The bell rang so loudly that it drowned out her next words and then the principal marched over and said, 'Off to class, girls. You can chat later.'

'We'll talk at recess,' Jade said, finally letting go of my arm.

I knew what that meant. She'd move very quickly from talking to threatening. How was I going to get out of this? As I joined Lucy, who was moving towards the steps, she said, 'How come you never said anything before?'

Because today was my day for being a complete moron! 'Mum won't say yes, that's why. I told you: she's got a bad leg.'

'Oh.' Her face cleared. 'But if she only has to stand and watch –'

I felt like I was a castle under siege and I wished for a huge, deep moat around myself. 'It's not going to happen, Lucy. Trust me.'

Lucy sniffed. 'Fine. Be like that, then.'

I could almost hear the little wheels turning and squeaking inside her head and by the time we reached our classroom and were sitting at our desks, her face had a cheesy smile on it. She leaned sideways. 'You haven't forgotten about showing me the dance steps, have you?' she said.

I closed my eyes for a moment, trying to ignore the irritation that bubbled up from my stomach. I clenched my hands and then made them lie flat on my desk. 'No, I haven't forgotten,' I said sweetly.

CHAPTER 13

The school day droned on and it was great to have PE after lunch and play coordination ball games for an hour, which warmed everyone up but reminded me of Ricky. If I walked home the long way, past the shops, maybe I'd see him.

Sure enough, he was sitting outside the milk bar, but he wasn't alone. Two older boys stood over him and Ricky hugged his basketball like a shield.

'Don't be a smartarse,' one of the boys said, whacking Ricky across the side of his head. His hands glittered with several large rings.

'Oww! Whadidya do that for?' Ricky cringed away from him.

I just stood there. What was I going to do? Leave? Yell out? I couldn't walk away and let him be beaten up. No way. I made myself walk towards them; my legs felt so rubbery I thought they were going to buckle and I'd collapse on the footpath.

'Think this loser needs a good smack around,' the other boy said. His face had several big white-headed pimples erupting from his greasy skin and a wispy goatee hung from his chin like a bit of fluff.

When I was closer, I squeaked, 'Hi, Ricky.'

The two boys swung around. 'Eeuuww, it's a little chicky come for Ricky,' the pimply boy sneered. Ricky peered at me as if he didn't recognise me.

'Who's this?' said RingFinger.

'Just someone I know,' Ricky mumbled.

'Who'd want to know you, turd-brain?'

'Leave her alone. She's okay.'

'Not if she's hanging around with a wuss like you,' Pimple said, laughing.

RingFinger grabbed Ricky by the neck of his T-shirt and almost lifted him off the ground. 'Tomorrow – or else.'

'Yeah, yeah. Put me down. I heard ya.' Retrieving his T-shirt and yanking it straight, Ricky glared at RingFinger, who cocked his fingers and put one to Ricky's head. Then, punching each other on the arm and laughing, he and Pimple sauntered away.

Ricky collapsed onto the bench. 'Hey, how's it going?'

I sat next to him. 'Scary,' I said. 'I thought they were going to bash you really badly.'

'Nah.' He sniffed. 'Mum'd have a fit if Con did that.'

'*Con?* You know him?'

'Yeah, that dude was my brother.'

'What was he threatening you for?'

'School.' He kicked at the concrete kerb with one shoe. 'Mum's been packing it that the welfare guy at the school reported me for not going. So she sent Con to have a word.'

'How many days did you miss?'

'Dunno. About ten.'

'This year?'

'This month.' He grinned. 'Don't like school. Can't see the point.'

I tried to get my head around someone who just didn't go to school. 'Don't you want to get a good job when you finish?'

Ricky burst out laughing and slapped his leg. 'Oh man, you kill me. I'm either going to end up unemployed or have some pathetic job like sweeping streets. Going to school isn't going to change that.'

'But –' I knew Orrin didn't like school either and he didn't get good marks, but he still went. Even Tam worked hard at school, because he needed maths and stuff for blacksmithing. I couldn't get a grip on someone who had given up so soon and was already expecting an awful life with no decent job.

'Hey, no sweat. I don't think about the future. No point.'

'I feel like I can't *not* think about it.'

'How do you mean?'

'For me, everything's about ballet, you know, trying to get into the Ballet School and dance for – for a career, I guess.'

'What – you're going to be in the Australian Ballet and be famous, like that Nureyev woman?'

Heat rushed up into my face. Was he having a go at me? 'That'd be a bit hard. Nureyev's a guy,' I said, trying to make a joke out of it.

'Nah, serious now. Is that what you're gonna do?' He stared at me, waiting for my answer, which made me feel a bit silly, as if I was talking about trekking to the South Pole or swimming Bass Strait. Maybe that was how Ricky saw it.

'Um . . . yeah. I hope so.'

'Hey, that is awesome!' His eyes sparkled. 'Are you any good?'

'I hope so.' I felt the thick cracking paint on the bench under my fingertips like a crocodile's skin. 'I have to be, I guess, but practice is a huge part of it. That's why I need the hall. Hey, I used the room last night. Thanks for helping me with it.'

His gaze dropped and a pink flush crept into his face. 'Would you . . . show me one day, you know, how you dance?'

'Sure. You want to learn?'

'Hey, calm down! Me – dance? As if.'

'I've seen you on the basketball court. You move like a dancer.'

Now his face was bright red. 'No way, man. You're joking.'

'I'm not. Listen, I had a favour to ask you anyway. Maybe . . .'

'What? What's the favour?'

'I need someone to help me stow away the tables and put them back again after practice. Dad can't do it because he's usually at work. Could you help? Not all the time, just now and then.'

He shrugged. 'Can't do it, my friend. I'm banned from the hall.'

'Oh.' How could I dance around the tables? And I couldn't expect Mum or Dad to take time off work to help me. They were doing enough for me already. I thought hard. 'There's a big sliding window in that room. Could you climb in the window and help me?'

'You sure do ask big favours,' he said.

'After we move the tables, you could practise with me.'

'I don't know any ballet.'

'Yeah, but you could learn. I'd show you.' What was I saying? I'd decided to keep it all a secret from Lucy so I wouldn't have her disrupting me, and now I was offering to teach Ricky, who knew nothing? But Dad often said that teaching someone was a good way to work it out for yourself. Besides, I wanted to do something for Ricky, something that wasn't about making him go to school or do stuff he hated.

I remembered something else that Orrin said. 'You know, some professional footballers and basketball players learn things like dance and yoga. It's supposed to be good for balance and flexibility and stuff.'

'Oh yeah, I'm headed for pro basketball. Not!' He poked me in the arm. 'Okay, you sold me. I'll help, but if that bald guy at the hall catches me in there, I'll be dead meat.'

'I'll stick something in front of the door so he can't get in.'

'Man, you got an answer for everything.' He held his hand up to high-five me and this time I whacked it so hard he laughed.

'I'd better go,' I said. 'See you outside the window just after four tomorrow?'

'Sure. Whatever.'

At home, it was lino time and with Mum's mirror, I could check my positions to make sure everything was perfect. The silver cord, from top to toe, pulled me up from the floor. I imagined Ricky doing these exercises with me and giggled. It'd be interesting, but I had to remember what I was there for – the audition!

'Brynna!' It was Mum. 'Pack up now, please.' She sounded really tired and, when I went inside, her face was drawn and pale.

'Are you okay, Mum?'

'It was crazy in there today. I'm knackered and my leg's killing me.' She sighed. 'Still, I guess I'd better do those exercises after dinner.'

'Why don't you have a shower and I'll do the potatoes and stuff?'

Her face brightened. 'Thanks, sweetie. That'd be great. I'll do the chicken later. Orrin's got footy training tonight, so it'll be the three of us at the table. Three. This family gets smaller every day.'

'Have you heard from Tam?' I said, as I pulled potatoes out of the bag under the sink.

'No, not a word. Typical. I might ring him tonight.'

She sorted through the mail on the bench. 'Another bill. I'm not opening that one.'

Mum's mobile phone trilled out the *Star Wars* theme. She talked for a few minutes and I worked out it was her boss. 'No, not for two weeks. I can't afford to push it too soon, Letty. Sorry.' She pressed the disconnect button and shrugged. 'They're keen, those girls, but they'll have to play without me for a while longer.'

'Mm-hmm,' I said and my stomach twisted into a knot again. I didn't want to ask Mum about coaching Jade's netball team – I was worried she'd say yes, just to make me happy and to make Jade my friend. But I didn't want Jade as a friend. I had to ask in a way that made it clear I wanted Mum to say no.

'It's funny that you used to coach,' I said.

'Why's that?' She sat down and started to pull off her socks. I fetched the liniment for her and she said, 'Thanks, I'll put that on after my shower.'

'Some of the girls at school play netball and their coach just broke her leg. She was snow skiing.'

'Ouch,' said Mum. 'Bet that hurt.'

'They – some of the girls – had this dumb idea that you could coach them. But,' I added quickly, 'I told them you couldn't. I said that already. That your leg was – you know –'

Mum glanced at me, folding her socks over into a soft ball, her mouth twitching. 'Well, I could think about it, I suppose. My leg is getting better.'

'You said it was really painful tonight!' I felt the edge

of the sink digging into my back and stepped forward. 'Plus, I already said no.'

Mum's eyebrows arched up. 'Is something going on, Brynna? You seem a bit uptight about it.'

'It's fine,' I said. 'They'll get someone else.' I grabbed a potato and the peeler. 'Go and have your shower, Mum.'

She went off to the bathroom and I heard the water running, but I had a feeling the topic was going to come up again, sooner or later. Why didn't I want her to coach Jade's team? It wasn't about me playing – nobody was going to force me to do that – so what was my problem with it?

CHAPTER 14

The next day, as I expected, Jade and Taylor ignored me, but Lucy hung with me, wanting help with the dance steps. I showed her a few times on the smooth concrete near the library, but by the end of lunchtime, she still didn't have them in the right sequence. I wrote them down for her, hoping that would be enough. In my head, I was already at the youth hall, dancing in the back room, and I rushed there as soon as school finished, even though I was early.

I wasn't sure Ricky would be outside the window at four, but after I'd jammed the door shut with a chair, there he was, gesturing to me to unlock and open the slider.

'You sure Baldy's not getting in?' he said.

'Not unless he's Superman.'

We folded the tables and put them aside, then I started my barre work. Ricky prowled round the room, looking under chairs and mats, checking outside the window, taking no notice of me. At first I was distracted, then I got used to him and focused on what I was doing. Centre exercises next, then the dance steps. Over and over, gradually getting faster.

'Don't you get sick of doing the same stuff all the time?'

His voice gave me a start. I'd forgotten he was there.

'Not really. You kind of centre yourself, start to feel what your body's doing and then it all flows.'

'Mmhh.' He didn't sound convinced.

'Are you going to have a go or not?' I asked.

'Nah, too hard.'

'I could do with some help. I'm going to practise pirouettes.'

'Pirra-whats?' He was lying across three chairs and sat up with a clatter, knocking one over.

'Pirouettes. Turns. Watch.' I moved to fifth position and completed a pirouette. 'The best dancers can do lots, one after the other.'

'Don't you get dizzy?'

'You fix your eyes on one spot and turn to it. Come on, have a go.' I pointed at his runners. 'You'll have to take them off. Your feet aren't smelly, are they?'

'What? You insulting me?'

'I've got two brothers, so I know all about smelly feet.'

'Where are they then? How come they don't fix the tables for you?' He slipped off his shoes and stepped into the centre of the room.

'Tam's gone back to Bendigo and Orrin trains for footy every night.' I nudged his foot with my toe. 'Put your feet like mine.'

He tried. 'Nah, this is silly.' He laughed.

'No, it's not. You just don't think you can do it.'

'Yes, I *can*.'

'Well, then. Like this.' I went through the pirouette slowly, showing him that his feet should end up in the same position and his arms should be curved down in front of him. Then I let him have a go on his own. And he did it almost perfectly first time.

My mouth fell open. 'Whoa. How did you do that? Nobody does it right the first few times. They overbalance usually.'

He shrugged. 'Dunno. Does this make me the next Nureyev?'

'Not yet. Do it again.'

So he did – several times – and he hardly teetered at all. Even his arms were nearly correct.

'Seriously, you should have lessons,' I said.

His face went pink. 'Oh yeah, I can just see my mates loving that.'

'Male ballet dancers are usually beating girls off them.'

'Really?' He twirled round. 'Might be worth it, then. If I could afford it.'

'You can always practise with me, but you'd have to do all of it, right from the warm-up.' I wondered if he would. 'Come on, let's pirouette together, across the room. I can fit four into the space, but you might only do three. You've got longer legs.'

The fact that he was watching and following me made me concentrate better on my own turns, and I managed four without a mistake. He finished just after me and said, 'Cool. So what were the steps you were doing before?'

'They're for my audition on Saturday, for a special class. I'll show you.'

We worked through the sequence, with me adjusting his arms and feet, counting the beats to stay together, repeating it until we were both dripping with sweat.

'Man, this is hard work,' he said.

'Yep, but the party's over. It's five-thirty.' I wiped my face with my towel, then threw it to him. 'Better put the tables back before that guy comes and tells me off for going over time.'

We soon had things back to normal, then Ricky climbed through the window and met me out the front. 'You want to practise with me on Friday – the whole lot?'

'Maybe, maybe not,' he said, but from his voice I knew he'd be there. He walked me to the corner of my street. 'Cool – see ya Friday.'

He ambled off, bouncing his basketball, and I arrived home just as Dad pulled into the driveway. I wondered if he'd seen me with Ricky, but he didn't say anything – just asked if I'd managed the tables all right and I said yes, someone helped me. I didn't want him worrying about me again.

After dinner, Mum lay on the floor in the lounge, going through all her leg exercises, and I read in my room. The book I'd chosen for my school review was boring, but it was too late to pick another one. Maybe I could write a review about why I hated it. Reason One: it wasn't about ballet! There was a light knock at my door and Mum came in. 'Phone for you. Lucy someone.'

I jumped up. 'Lucy is in my class at school, and she goes to Ms Ellergren's, too.'

When I picked up the phone, Lucy said, 'I still can't get those steps right, you know, for Saturday.' I could hear tears in her voice. 'Can you please go through them a couple more times with me tomorrow?'

'Yeah, sure,' I said. 'We can do it at lunchtime.'

'Oh, that'd be great,' Lucy said. 'See you then.'

I hung up. 'Is she in the netball team, too?' Mum said.

'No, she's like me. She doesn't want to play competition games in case she gets hurt and can't go to ballet classes.'

'So who's in this team then?' Mum was picking at her nail polish – something she did when she was thinking through a decision. The last thing I wanted was her coaching Jade's team, but if she thought I was being nasty, she'd be upset with me.

'It's just a school team,' I said at last. 'Nothing special. But there's one girl in it who is really fanatical. Like, she's always mad at me and Lucy for not playing and she's – mean about it.'

'Oh,' Mum said. 'That's a shame. You know what I feel about attitude and how important it is.'

'You're going to say no, aren't you?'

She jerked round to face me. 'Probably. I might call the school, or I might not. I'll see how my leg is by the end of the week.' She stretched her arms above her head. 'Time for a cuppa and a quiet sit in front of the telly, I think.'

After she'd gone, I kept thinking about the netball team. Maybe my whole problem with it was Jade. If Mum did decide to coach the team (please, no!), I'd see a lot more of Jade and I didn't trust her.

Was Lucy like Jade? Would she only hang with me as long as I helped her with the dance steps? What would she do when I turned up at the class try-out on Saturday? Why couldn't I be honest with her? I was such a wuss sometimes! I promised myself that I'd tell her as soon as I could. I had to.

At lunchtime the next day, Lucy and I found a quiet spot in the corridor outside the library and I showed her the steps yet again. She followed me as I went through them first, then I watched as she did them on her own. She made a couple of slips and I thought her feet positions needed correcting, but she was a thousand times better than the day before.

After a small stumble, she said, 'I'll get it right by Saturday. I will. Don't you think?'

I swallowed hard; my mouth was dry. 'You've improved lots. It's nearly perfect. And – I'll be there, too, so I'll, you know, be able to cheer you on.'

She stopped mid-step, her head shooting up, her mouth turning down. 'I thought you weren't allowed to try out.'

'Um, well, Mum changed her mind. But she said I

wasn't to get my hopes up.' I couldn't hold her gaze – her eyes were like bullets. 'Okay, let's go over the steps again.'

'What's the point?' she snapped. 'It's obvious you'll get into the class and I won't.'

Heat rolled up my neck and into my face. Yep, Lucy was just like Jade, but I wasn't going to let her pull me down. 'Hey, don't tell me you've been sucked in to what Stephanie said. You're better than them. You just have to get in there and show them. And Ms Ellergren.'

'You think so?' Her face had transformed from furious to hopeful. She was as desperate to make the class as I was, but if she couldn't get the dance steps right, she was going to have no hope. I tried hard to keep that thought from showing.

'Sure. You know that practice is 95 per cent of what it takes. The Silhouettes have probably done ten minutes' worth, if that.'

'Yeah, probably,' she said. 'I'll go over everything again tonight, at home. That'll make all the difference.'

'It sure will.'

'Can I ask you something?'

I nodded. I wondered what was coming. Not the netball team, please.

'What does your mum think about your ballet? Like – your future.'

I folded my arms. I wasn't sure how much to tell her or how much I'd already revealed. 'She wants me to do well, to – achieve what I want, I guess.'

'What would you say if I told you –' She scuffed her shoe along the floor. 'My mum thinks I'm wasting my time.'

'But she pays for your classes at Ms Ellergren's,' I said.

'She'd pay for me to learn piano, or do art classes, or even stupid yoga, if I wanted.'

'What are you on about?'

'I want to audition for the National Ballet School. Mum says it's a waste of time. But I'm going to anyway, even if she says no. I *have* to.' Her voice was so intense and serious that I didn't know what to say. 'It's my secret,' she went on. 'You're not allowed to tell anyone.'

'I won't.' This absolutely was not the right time for me to tell her my special dream.

'Mum doesn't think I'm good enough. She says stuff like, "Don't be too disappointed if you don't make it" and "If you set your sights too high, you'll fall an awfully long way". It's like she's already decided I haven't got a chance and she's trying to prepare me.' A tear dribbled down her face and she brushed it away roughly.

'I'm sorry,' I said. I had no idea what else to say.

Lucy chewed on her thumbnail. 'I'll do what you said – I'll practise all night tonight and every possible moment. Then I'll get it perfect. And Ms Ellergren will tell Mum I'm good enough to audition.' She straightened up and smiled at me hopefully.

The bell saved me from having to say any more.

CHAPTER 15

It was lino practice night, but the wind in the garage whistled through the door gap and swirled around like invisible snow. I shivered and headed back to the lounge room, but it was too hard to get my feet to move on the carpet, so I pushed the kitchen table to one side and did the exercises there, in front of Mum's mirror. Once I'd warmed up, it was a good opportunity to check my head and arm positions. And I remembered something I'd read once – to get your arms moving correctly, pretend you're swimming in peanut butter! That was fun to imagine and it helped.

Mum came home just as I was finishing with arabesques; you needed grace and balance for them. A silver cord.

'Lovely,' she said. 'Pity our kitchen's so small.'

She helped me put the table back and sat down. 'I've been thinking about your netball team.'

'It's not my team! I don't want to play.' I tugged at the ribbons on my shoes, and one immediately went into a knot. 'Stupid thing!' I muttered, pulling harder and making it worse.

'Here, let me,' Mum said. She crouched down next to me and picked at the knot with fingers that were so rough they snagged on the satin. Finally, the knot unravelled. 'There.' As she stood up again, she groaned. 'That'll teach me. I need to work on my flexibility, don't I?'

'Try yoga,' I said, untying my other ribbon more carefully.

'I thought I'd quite like to coach again,' she said. 'And a school team wouldn't be too tough or competitive.'

'Don't you believe it,' I said. 'Jade's like a bulldozer: she won't stop for anything.'

Mum tilted her head from side to side. 'Yeah, she'd be a challenge. But if someone doesn't teach her now how to behave on the court, she'll never make it later on.'

'Who cares? She's rude and aggro and I wouldn't play against her if you paid me.'

'That's not like you.'

Mum was doing her be-nice-to-everyone-and-they'll-be-nice-to-you act, but I didn't buy it anymore. 'She's not like anyone I know, Mum. She's –' I couldn't think of a word I was allowed to use. 'Awful.' That barely covered it.

'I haven't decided yet,' she said. 'So don't say anything at school. I'll make my mind up tomorrow, after I've watched them. All right?'

'I don't care,' I muttered. 'I'm not playing.' But it burned me that Mum would give her time and energy to someone like Jade, despite what I'd said. If Mum wanted to coach someone, why didn't she coach – well, Ricky? That idea hit me like a kick in the head and I opened my mouth to suggest it. But what was the point? Ricky didn't have a team to play in – he was just messing around on the court by himself. Where would coaching get him?

I didn't know enough about him, either, but I vowed to find out as soon as I could.

Mum had rearranged the chairs, unaware of the ideas spinning through my head. 'Now, let's get cracking with dinner,' she said. 'Orrin will want something hot when he finishes tonight. It's cold enough out there to snow. And Tam's ringing later to tell us how he's going.'

I changed out of my ballet gear and went back to the kitchen, stirred a pot of soup while Mum grilled chops, and watched the peas and carrots swimming round in the brown mix. Why wasn't Ricky playing for another team? Surely losing a venue wouldn't stop him? Maybe it was a territory thing and no one else wanted him. My brain skipped on to Lucy, and I visualised her feet moving through the dance steps, stumbling, in the wrong position. No, it was practice – she was committed. She said so. And if she did well on Saturday, she'd make it into the class and convince her mum.

Who was I kidding? The awful feeling in my stomach was right. Lucy wasn't going to be in the class. Maybe I wasn't either. After all, why should I get in?

Because I was determined to be chosen, that was why. I'd dance till I dropped for Ms Ellergren, if that was what it would take!

I gave the soup another big stir for luck.

When Ricky climbed through the window the following afternoon, I thought he'd chickened out of dancing with me. He wore a blue puffy jacket and a bulky sweatshirt, with huge thick-soled runners on his feet and I couldn't see him moving at all in those clothes. But once we'd moved the tables, he took off the jacket and runners and grinned at me.

'Hey, I wasn't gonna wear skinny little tights on the way here. Apart from the fact that they'd freeze my you-know-whats off, my mates'd all cack themselves laughing if they saw me.' He lifted his sweatshirt. 'See? T-shirt. And my socks can come off if they're too slippery.'

'Okay. Cool,' I said. 'Let's warm up.'

He stood behind me, slightly to one side with one hand on a chair like me, and I talked him through what I was doing. I wasn't going to correct him like Ms Ellergren did or we'd be there all night. I went through the feet positions and arm positions and then, with each exercise, I told him where arms and legs should be and left it up to him to follow. Every now and then I turned around, but each time he seemed to be doing the movements correctly, if a bit awkwardly.

'I feel like a girl,' he said.

'Trust me, you don't look like one,' I said. As his body warmed up, he'd taken off his sweatshirt and he definitely wasn't a skinny weed. 'Now, centre exercises.'

'When do we get to dance?'

'Soon. You've got to warm up properly, especially in the cold weather, or you can injure yourself.'

'Okay, Ms Teacher.'

From the centre, we went on to pirouettes. To my horror, I overbalanced on the second turn and stopped abruptly in the middle, so that Ricky nearly bumped into me.

'Hey, you're supposed to keep going!'

'I did it wrong,' I muttered.

'So fix it,' he said. 'Come on.'

We went back to the side of the room and started again. This time I waited, took a couple of breaths and concentrated on feeling where my body was, what was out of line, and on flowing up, around and down. One, two, three, four. Perfect!

I watched Ricky behind me, completing three before he hit the wall on the other side. 'Not enough room,' he said.

'Do them in the one spot. Like this.' I showed him how to pirouette without taking big steps forward. It always seemed harder to me to do it that way. He did five before he had to stop, shaking his head.

'Dizzy. Forgot to look at one place, like you said.'

I shook my head. 'You are amazing. You did all of those without overbalancing or anything.'

'Cool, huh?' He beamed. 'It's basketball, see, moving the ball around and jumping and stuff.'

'That's not all it is. You catch on really fast, and you get the arms and feet positions, too. Most beginners take forever to put them together.'

He shrugged. 'How about those dance steps now?'

We went through the sequence from Ms Ellergren's six times, and I wished I had music to dance it to.

'What next?' he said.

'That's all she showed us. That's all I need to do for Saturday.'

'Yeah, but –' He frowned. 'There must be more. What would you do next? What steps would you add?'

That stopped me for a few moments. 'I'm not sure. Um –' I thought about what we'd done so far. Here, I'd been wishing for music, but what music would go with steps like these? Not *Swan Lake*. Maybe something lighter like *The Nutcracker*, which was Tchaikovsky. I hummed some of it softly. Yes, that worked.

'Maybe something like this?' I said. Still humming, I danced the first steps, then added more – petit allegro, an arabesque – trying things out until I found steps that fitted together and flowed. I tried my sequence again, adding a couple of things. 'How did that look?' I said.

'Hey, how would I know? Good, I guess. It matched the first bit.'

'Come on, then, follow me.'

'Yes, ma'am.'

We danced the full sequence twice and then collapsed on our chairs.

'This dancing thing's hard,' he said. 'Worse than PE at school.'

'Errm, school. Does that mean you're going?'

He pulled at his bottom lip. 'Yeah, worse luck. What good's learning about the environment gonna do me? I'm not gonna be a scientist.'

'Don't you want to know why we've got global warming? Or what you can do about it?'

'What difference does it make? We've got water restrictions. I've got to bucket shower water out to Mum's garden. That's bad enough, without seeing a million photos of pollution and melting glaciers.'

I couldn't figure out how to convince him that if everyone knew about global warming and, more importantly, cared, maybe we could do something. I thought about it as we put the tables back and when we met outside to walk home, I said, 'Where does your family come from?'

'Here.'

'No – your father, grandfather and great-grandfather.'

He laughed sourly. 'Mum'd just like to know where Dad is *now* – never mind where he came from!'

'Come on, tell me. Where?'

'Grandad came from Italy. He always had his homemade grappa happening. That stuff'd blow your head off.' He glanced at me. 'Why're you asking?'

'I was just curious. You know about where I come from.' It was much easier to talk to Ricky than Lucy and ask questions like this. He was so straightforward.

I huddled down into my coat and tucked my hands deeper into my pockets. Big drops of rain started to fall and splattered on the footpath. 'Maybe your great-grandfather was a famous dancer and you never knew about it.'

'As if.' He laughed, then he was silent and I wondered if he really was thinking about it, or whether he was more worried about getting wet. We reached the corner of my street and he pulled his jacket hood over his head.

'Hey, listen, you kill 'em in that audition.'

'I'll try.'

'You do more than try.' He pointed his index finger at me. 'You blitz them.'

'Yes, sir.' I saluted and laughed, and watched as he ran off, trying to get out of the rain before it really pelted down. I jammed my backpack under my arm and raced to my own house, arriving just as the big drops turned into a downpour. No way Ricky was going to make it home in time. I hoped he'd found a big tree or a doorway.

CHAPTER 16

Saturday. The big day. The try-out for the class. I woke with a queasy feeling in my stomach. Was I coming down with a bug? No, it was nerves. Get up and get going, I told myself. Move past the nerves. Make them work for you.

But the feeling wouldn't go away and turned into a hideous rolling every time I thought about it. When I sat down for breakfast, Mum took one look at me and said, 'Nerves, huh?'

I nodded.

'Thought so. You'll be fine.'

My cereal looked like a white lake filled with yellow lumps. Yuck. I took a breath. I had to know before I went to Ms Ellergren's. 'Mum, if I get into the class, will I be able to do it? You know – can we afford it?'

She breathed deeply and my shoulders slumped. 'I – well, your dad seems to think we'll manage it. We're just stretched pretty tight at the moment because of moving, and uniforms and things at your new schools.' She sighed. 'But with Tam gone, there's one less to feed, and he did eat a lot.'

'But I didn't want him to –' Guilt crawled through me again. First I made Tam come here when he didn't want to, and now his going away meant we could afford my extra classes. I poked at my cereal.

'Cheer up,' Mum said. 'Let's work it out when you're accepted into the class.'

At least she'd said *when*, not *if*. Not like Lucy's mum, who was probably already planning something to cheer Lucy up when she wasn't picked.

Soon, we were on our way to class. We'd left in plenty of time so we wouldn't have to rush or be late. Mum knew that would set my nerves off again. I was first in the changing room and sat there, eyes closed, breathing in and out slowly, focusing on calm.

'Praying won't help.'

My eyes flew open and there was Stephanie, dressed perfectly as usual in tight jeans and heeled boots. Her jacket had a ruff of fur around the collar – she looked like something out of a Christmas Disney movie.

'I wasn't praying.'

'You should be.'

'Oh, get stuffed,' I said. It wasn't very original, but it made her flush and she turned away with a sniff. Within a few minutes, the changing room was full of chattering girls – most of them going on about how nervous they were. I escaped to the studio and waited by the barre for Ms Ellergren to start the class. Lucy joined me, looking flustered. She was still tying her hair up.

'My mum would have to be late today, of all days,' she whispered.

Ms Ellergren banged her stick on the floor and the class began.

Two hours later, after the reverence or curtsey, we were allowed half an hour's break before the audition. Most of the others raced out to the nearest fast food shops, but Mum had packed me a thick egg sandwich and some juice. I sat in the changing room and forced the food down, knowing I'd need the energy after the long, tiring class.

Then it was time. I was surprised to see that nearly every girl and boy in my class was there – were they *all* planning to audition for the NBS? We lined up in the centre of the studio and waited.

Ms Ellergren walked up and down, looking at each one of us as she talked. 'I rarely run a special class like this, but that is for a good reason. I'm not just looking for those who will audition next month for the National Ballet School. I'm looking for total commitment and dedication. You will have to attend two extra classes per week, as well as your normal Saturday class. You will not be allowed to miss a single class, unless –' a tiny smile curved on her mouth, 'you get run over by a bus.' A few girls giggled, then hushed again.

I definitely had the commitment and dedication part.

She clapped her hands. 'You have heard what it is going to be, what is required. Some of you may wish to leave now. If so, away you go.'

Nobody moved.

'Very well. I will watch four of you at a time.' She quickly divided us into fours and, with Mimi playing the piano, each group was taken through a series of exercises, some of which we'd never done before. She made us do arabesques, jumps and pirouettes, and I was so glad that I'd practised hard all week. My pirouettes felt as close to perfect as I could get them, but Ms Ellergren never said a word, or even smiled.

Finally, we got to the sequence of steps she'd given us. At that point, she sent us all outside and we had to dance alone. I stood in the foyer, my eyes glued to the picture of Ms Ellergren in *Swan Lake*, while everyone flexed and bent, staying warm as we waited. The Silhouettes kept to themselves in one corner, with their backs to us. That was fine by me. Lucy stood alone, her face miserable, her eyes closed. She looked like she was counting silently and I guessed she was going over the steps yet again.

'Brynna.' My turn. I wiped my hands with my towel and went in.

'The steps, please.'

I knew them so well that I could focus on flow and grace and avoid rushing the sequence and messing it up.

'Good,' she said. 'Now, Mimi will play some music for you. I want you to dance the steps to the music, then keep going. Create your own steps; show me how you would continue the dance.'

One part of me was astonished – I'd never been in an audition like this before. Usually people only wanted to see perfection in what you'd learnt. Another part of me said *Thanks, Ricky*. I'd already had a go at this because of him.

I waited for the music to start, and danced. Most of the steps I'd worked out fell into place almost perfectly, some of the jumps not so well, and when the music continued, I repeated the first sequence.

'Excellent. Thank you. I will let you know by Sunday evening whether you've been selected or not.'

'Thank you, Ms Ellergren.' I curtseyed low and left. It was over!

Lucy grabbed me as I passed through the foyer. 'What do you have to do? Is it just the steps? Please tell me.' Her face was dismal and I didn't know what to say. Was it cheating to tell her? But someone else had overheard and said, 'Lucy, that's not fair. Everyone has to be even.'

'Sorry,' I said, and headed for the changing room.

Outside, I fell into the front seat of our car, my arms and legs suddenly all floppy. 'How did it go?' Mum said.

'I've got no idea. I felt like I danced well, but –'

'Did all your extra practice help?'

'Yes, and it was amazing. This dance sequence she told us to learn, well, I've been working on that and yesterday Ricky asked me what would come next, so I sort of worked out these steps, and that's exactly what Ms Ellergren wanted me to do. It was so weird – like he could see into my future – and it really helped.'

Mum looked a bit taken aback. 'Who's Ricky?'

'Um, a friend. You know.'

'From school?'

'No, he's from round here. He's been helping me with the tables at the youth hall.' I was terrified that she'd ask if she could meet him.

'I see. Does he dance, too?'

'No.' My brain zinged back to the idea I'd had before. 'But he plays basketball and he's really good. He's the kind of person you could coach and he'd be a superstar.'

Mum's mouth twitched. 'In your expert opinion.'

'Yeah. But – he doesn't play in a team right now. Their basketball stadium burned down.'

'Oh, that's a shame.'

I waited for her to say more, but she just started the car. I wasn't going to push it, because I might accidentally end up convincing her to coach Jade's team instead. No way was that going to happen! Besides, I had the special class to worry about. Even more than that, Ms Ellergren had reminded me that the NBS audition was only weeks away. Once it had felt like years; suddenly, it loomed awfully close. For few moments, panic flickered through me and I closed my eyes, trying to will it away.

With the class try-out over, the rest of Saturday and all day Sunday took as long to pass as I expected – forever. I'd missed Orrin's footy game, but his team had won again and he'd played the full four quarters and kicked five goals. On Sunday, he was off to a local gym to work out. Lucky him, to have his training to fill in time. The last thing I wanted to do was ballet. My body felt like a saggy jumping castle. On

Sunday, Mum took one look at my gloomy face and decided that she and Dad and I were going to the movies. There was a comedy on and even Dad laughed instead of groaning like he usually did, and we ate pizza afterwards.

I checked my watch every five minutes until Mum made me take it off. 'You're driving me nuts,' she said. We were home by five and then I had to wait. And wait. And wait.

Finally, around eight, the phone rang. I stared at it as if it was a snake.

'Answer it, please,' said Mum.

'Hello.'

'Is that Brynna?'

'Yes.'

'It's Ms Ellergren here.'

My body froze, and I stopped breathing. Was it going to be yes? Or no?

CHAPTER 17

Ms Ellergren kept talking, as if she had no idea I was nearly dying on this end of the line. 'I'm calling to tell you that you are one of the six selected for my class.'

'Oh.' It came out as a strangled squeak.

'Are you there? Did you hear me?' She sounded a bit annoyed.

'Yes. Thank you. Thank you so much.'

'You mightn't be thanking me soon,' she said, laughing. 'Now, can I speak to your mother, please?'

I handed the phone to Mum, then jumped up and down like a Mexican jumping bean until Mum grabbed my arm and made me sit.

'Yes, Ms Ellergren. Yes, that is a bit of a problem. I don't know. We'll have to talk about it here. Yes. Yes. That'd be helpful. Yes. Thanks. Goodbye.'

Problem? What problem?

Money. Her big frown was telling me that, right now. No money, no class. But just this morning, she'd said it might be possible! I slouched in the chair, feeling my excitement drain out of me like water from the bath. 'But I got in!' I said.

'I know.'

Dad came into the kitchen. 'Uh-oh, gloomy faces. Well, better luck next time, Brynnie.'

'It's not that, Dad. I was selected.'

He looked at Mum and raised his eyebrows. 'What are we up for? A million dollars a week?'

'Dad!' I hated him joking about something so important to me.

'Almost. She's making the classes longer, so the fee has increased.' Mum tapped her fingers on the table in a drum roll. 'She's offered us a way out. A deal. If we want it. It smacks of charity to me, and you know how I feel about that.'

'What did she say?' I asked.

'She needs someone to clean the studio twice a week. Her old cleaner's retired and she's offering the job to us – well, I guess that means me – in return for all of your class fees.'

'That'd work out great,' I said.

'Except that I'm so tired when I finish work, there's no way I can take on a cleaning job as well. And your dad's the same. We work long hours on our feet. The thought of cleaning that huge place – I can't do it.'

'I could do most of it,' I said. 'I wanted to get a job anyway.'

'You're twelve,' Dad said. 'It'd be too big a job for you. Mum's right: we couldn't cope.'

'So what are you saying?' I said. 'I can't be in the class, because we can't afford it, and I can't clean the studio to pay for it. What's the point, then? Why did we even bother moving down here?' I could hear my voice getting louder, but I couldn't stop. 'We made all those big changes, moved house, you got new jobs, we had to go to new schools – for what? For me? For my dancing? This class is my first big opportunity and I can't do it. Let's all go home right now.'

'Brynna!' Mum said.

'Go home?' Orrin had walked in behind Dad. 'I'm not going home. I'm on a roll!'

'Well, lucky you, then!' I snapped.

'What's the prob?' Orrin asked. 'Fill me in.'

Mum explained it to him while I sat, arms tightly crossed, fuming. Every time I tried to imagine telling Ms Ellergren I couldn't be in her class, my eyes filled with tears, then I'd blink hard and force them back.

'That's cool,' Orrin said. 'The cleaning'll pay for the classes, but none of you can do it. So why don't I do it?'

'You?' said Mum. 'You can't even keep your room clean.'

'Excuse me,' he said, 'that was Tam. My room's totally neat, now he's outta there.'

'Would you clean the studio for nothing? To help me?' I couldn't believe it.

'Nah, course not. But if Mum paid me what she's paying right now for your Saturday class, that'd do me. It'd save me looking for something else, which I'd been thinking about. The guy at the gym offered me a cleaning gig, but it's too sweaty and smelly there for me.' He grinned at all of us and spread his hands out. 'Is that a cool solution or what?'

'Super cool!' I said.

'I'd pay you more than that,' Mum said. 'It'd be worth it.'

'Majorly cool,' Orrin said. 'Okay, when's dinner?'

I could hardly eat, but Mum set a plate of pasta and cheese in front of me and a fork in my hand. My brain was working overtime, trying to imagine what the new classes would be like and how hard they'd be. Three classes a week! This was quite a step up. Before, I'd been so focused on getting picked, but now I could see that it had been the proof I'd wanted – that I truly was good enough. As well as the classes, I'd still be practising in the youth hall.

As I speared curly bits of pasta, I daydreamt about Ricky being in my ballet class. Would he hate the classical music, or would he prefer modern dance? Ms Ellergren didn't seem too interested in anything modern. I'd seen some fabulous male dancers on video and in movies, and Ricky seemed strong enough and graceful enough to be a very good artist.

But he'd have to really want to do it, not just have fun with me. Who knew what that might lead to? Maybe one day he'd come along to watch a class at Ms Ellergren's and decide to give it a go.

There was no point dreaming about it, though. As Mum said, my dream was not for everyone, and determination and passion had to play a big part, otherwise you just didn't stay the distance.

It was so hard to get to sleep after dinner. My brain zoomed back and forth, and ballet kept getting mixed up with the family stuff and school. My family had done so much for me, and sometimes I felt weighed down by the expectations and totally freaked out about the possibility of failing. But, as Mum said, we were all healthy, we had a place to live, some money (if not lots), and I had my dream. There were heaps of kids in the world who had none of that, who didn't even have a mum and dad to provide food, and it made me feel all mixed up. Was I supposed to feel guilty, or grateful? Or both?

Finally, I fell asleep and woke the next morning with a headache. On the way to school, I remembered Lucy and almost turned around and ran home again. I was sure she wouldn't have been selected – what was I going to say to her? There was no point pretending I hadn't been chosen.

When I reached our classroom and saw her there, crying, I stopped by the door and waited. What could I say? Obviously I was sorry, but was there anything that would make her feel better? Nothing I could think of.

Jade saw me waiting, glared at me and then whispered in Lucy's ear. Lucy turned to me, tears streaking her face, but she didn't ask. I nodded. I couldn't lie. Was Lucy going to burst into new tears?

But she sniffed loudly a couple of times, blew her nose and shrugged off Jade's arm. Then she came over to me. 'You really got in?'

'Yeah. Lucky, hey?'

'No, you deserved it. You're good.' She sighed. 'Do you think Stephanie was picked?'

'I sure hope not. She'll probably try to trip me, or run me over with her mum's 4WD.'

Lucy smiled a little, her chin wobbling. 'That's the down side, for sure.'

'I'm sorry you didn't get in,' I said.

'Mum was having a hissy fit over having to drive me to the extra classes anyway, so at least she's happy. What did your mum say?'

'The extra fees are our problem, but I think it'll work out.'

'Good luck,' she said, squeezing my arm, and happiness bubbled through me again.

I couldn't wait to see Ricky after school and, as soon as he'd climbed in the hall window, I grabbed him and swung him round. 'I made it, I got picked!' I said. 'And it was thanks to you.'

'Whoa, what'd I do?' He stood with his arms folded and eyeballed me.

'On Friday, you asked me what came next in the dance, remember? You said something else had to happen, to follow on, and I tried out more steps.'

'Yeah, so?'

'That is *exactly* what she asked me to do in the audition. And because I'd already done it for you, I could dance the steps for her.'

'Way to go,' he said, but his face wasn't happy at all.

'What's the matter? Aren't you pleased for me?'

'Sure. But with the extra classes, you won't be doing this anymore.' He gestured around the room. 'The practice thing.'

Aha! He thought I was going to ditch the youth hall and him, and he wouldn't be able to dance with me. 'No, I need to do this, too. Practice is important. Are you still going to help me and do it with me?'

'Yeah, I guess so. Why not?' he said, trying to sound like he didn't care much either way. But I knew he did.

'Let's get started then.'

We folded and moved the tables, then took off our jackets to start. I tied the ribbons on my ballet shoes and stood up, ready to begin with a chair, and suddenly noticed something different. Something that made my eyes bug out of my head!

CHAPTER 18

I stared down at Ricky's feet and couldn't help the big grin that spread across my face. 'You've got ballet shoes!'

He shrugged. 'No big deal. I didn't want to slip over, that's all. Anyway, they're not real ones.'

No, they weren't – they were the slip-on kind – but I kept my mouth shut. Shoes! Maybe he was getting a bit more serious about this.

We worked through barre and centre exercises, practised pirouettes, then I showed him a series of steps and jumps across the room. 'These are called glissades and petit allegro,' I said, demonstrating, 'and this is a jeté.'

'Why do they have different names?'

'It depends what position your feet are in and whether you start on one foot or two, or finish on a different foot.'

He looked puzzled. 'What do you call the really big jumps, then – the ones you see the guys do? You know, where they do turns in the air and stuff?'

'One is a grand jeté en tournant – that's where you do a big jump, turn in the air and land on the other foot. I can sort of show you, but like I said, women don't do the bigger jumps.' I made sure I had plenty of room, then, with a short run-up, I did a grand jeté for him.

'Where's the turn?'

'I'm not going to try that in here. I don't want to fall over and hurt myself – not now.'

'Can I have a go?'

'Sure.' But I wasn't sure at all. He was only a beginner – why did he want to try jumps that were so difficult? It was a boy thing, for sure. There had been two boys in Mrs Calzotti's class and they were always wanting to do bigger and more complicated jumps, but she wouldn't let them. Sometimes I'd get to class early and there they were, trying out all kinds of jumps before she arrived.

Ricky surprised me. He practised half a dozen grands jetés first, his face screwed up in concentration, and then he tried one with a turn. I gasped as he landed sideways, but he recovered and straightened up. 'I get it,' he said. 'Not like that. Turn earlier.' He wasn't talking to me! On the next try, he performed it almost perfectly and I shook my head.

'How did you do that?'

'Dunno. I just thought I needed to turn earlier, that's all.' He nudged me. 'Not making you jealous, am I? Sure you don't want me to take your place in that special class?'

'Seriously, you should go to a class. You'd be great.'

His whole face and neck turned red. 'Don't be going weird on me and trying to convert me to the *bell-ay* thing. I am the basketball king, not the Nureyev kid.'

'Yeah, sure,' I said, laughing. 'Let's pack up.'

A sharp knock on the door made me jump. 'Hello?' the bald man shouted through the door. 'Why is this door locked? Hello?'

'I'm outta here,' Ricky whispered and climbed out of the window headfirst.

I took the chair out from under the handle and opened the door. 'Sorry,' I said. 'The door kept flying open and annoying me.'

The bald man stared at me suspiciously. 'Who else was in here? I heard talking.'

'That was me. I have to count out loud for my dancing, you know, for the beats.'

He glanced around the room. 'You haven't put the tables back.'

'I've only just finished my practice,' I said. 'I'm going to do it now.'

'All right, then.' He checked out the room again, as if he was hoping to find something wrong, but the only wrong thing had already disappeared. 'See that you do.' He left and I hauled the first table out, laid it on the floor before unfolding it, then I couldn't stand it up because it was too heavy, so I left it there and unfolded the other one. Now what? There was no way I'd get them up on their legs without help and if I had to ask the bald man to give me a hand, I'd get in trouble.

I slid open the window, hoping Ricky was there, but he'd gone. 'Rats.' I had to lift the tables up somehow. I peered down the corridor and saw one of the TV couch potatoes heading for the toilet. When he came out, I said, 'Excuse me, can you give me a hand?'

'Whaffor?' He acted like I was asking him to rob a bank, his eyes moving sideways and back again.

'I need help putting two tables up.'

'Whaddever.'

To my surprise, he came and helped me lift them without another word.

'Thanks a million,' I said. 'I really appreciate it.' He hunched his shoulders slightly, smiled and went back to his TV. Phew!

I thought Ricky might be waiting for me near the park, but he really had gone, so I walked home, thinking about the first new class. Tomorrow at five. I'd have to catch a bus to get there, as Mum and Dad would still be at work, so I needed to find the bus stop and have money for a ticket. Would Mum pick me up? I hoped so. It'd be dark by the time class finished.

I wished I didn't have to go to school the next day, see Lucy again and have to console her while pretending I thought my place was no big deal, but there was a surprise waiting for me. Jade had persuaded Lucy to play netball in her team after all.

'What about ballet?' I said.

Lucy twisted a curl round her finger and avoided my eyes. 'If I'm not in the class, Mum won't let me audition for the NBS, so what's the point of worrying about getting hurt in netball?'

'But you can't give up,' I said. 'Anything might happen.'

'Like what?' she spat the words at me. 'Darling Stephanie might fall down and break her leg? Hardly. Mum was right – I shouldn't have got my hopes up. I'll keep going to class on Saturday, but I'm not going to give up everything else – not when I'm not good enough.'

'But –' I wanted to tell her that if she gave up, then no, she wouldn't ever be good enough, but her face was closed and sullen and I could see I'd be wasting my time. 'You might change your mind,' I said lamely.

Jade came over and hooked her arm through Lucy's. 'The team will win for sure with you, Luce.' She narrowed her eyes at me. 'I suppose you won't even come to watch us play.'

'When's the game?' I said.

Jade let out an exaggerated sigh. 'Geez, we've only been talking about it for two weeks. It's this afternoon, after school.'

'Um – I can't. I've got ballet class.'

The sneer I expected slid across Jade's face. 'Yes, you go off and do your fancy tippy-toes stuff. We don't need you anyway.' She pulled at Lucy's arm and they walked away. Lucy didn't even look back at me.

Fine. I was used to it. And if Mum volunteered to coach them, I'd never speak to her again. I spent the day on my own and sat in the library, trying to read the rest of the book for my assignment. I'd written the review without finishing the story and I knew Mrs Nguyen would ask me more questions. But all I could think about was the class and who else would be in it. Lucy seemed sure that Stephanie had been picked. Maybe it would be the Silhouettes and me!

But there were a couple of others in our Saturday class, including one of the boys, who were excellent dancers. As the bell rang, I skimmed the last few pages in the book and shoved it in my bag. I was right – Mrs Nguyen did quiz me on it, but I managed to answer her questions without looking too stupid.

Time dragged and then rushed in bursts. When I arrived at the studio, it was like my first day there all over again. Shaky legs, brain full of fuzz, stomach churning. I went into the changing rooms to take off my top layer of clothes and put my ballet shoes on. Lost inside my nerves, I barely noticed when the door opened.

'Oh, that's just lovely.' Stephanie stood in front of me, hands on her hips, lip curled. 'We're going to be dancing with a cow. *Clip-clop*.'

Behind her was Danielle. Nobody else. That answered my question about the Silhouettes. Danielle stared at me with a face like marble. 'How did you get in?'

'Same as you,' I said.

'Obviously everyone else was hopeless, then,' Stephanie said. She moved towards me and I quickly tucked my feet under the bench.

The door opened again and two more girls rushed in, their faces pink and excited. Antoinette and Kate, the two I thought had the best chance of being picked. They grinned at me. 'How cool is this?' Kate said.

Stephanie made a big production out of sighing and shaking her head, like she couldn't believe she had to be in the class with such a bunch of moronic amateurs. Antoinette made a face behind her back and we giggled.

Someone rapped on the door. 'Come on, stop yabbering. Ms Ellergren's waiting.' It was David, the boy whose grace I'd admired – he'd been picked, too. We all scuttled out of the changing room and into the studio, where Ms Ellergren stood, checking her watch. I knew it wasn't five o'clock yet, but that didn't matter.

'Not good enough,' Ms Ellergren snapped. 'I expect you here before five, warming up, ready to begin. Make a note. Lateness will not be tolerated.'

Oops. At least we were all off to a bad start together. Ms Ellergren allowed us time to stretch and flex and then we launched into barre exercises that went on and on forever. There was no music from Mimi – it was all the basics, while Ms Ellergren walked up and down, up and down, adjusting everyone's positions by millimetres, moving hands, heads, feet, until I wanted to scream. I kept telling myself it was army drill and we just had to drum it in and get it perfect. But as my legs and arms ached and then burned, and sweat drenched my leotard, it took everything I had to keep going after the perfection she demanded.

Finally, it was over. An hour and a half had felt like three days. Everyone's faces mirrored my own, I was sure.

Pale with exhaustion, shadowed eyes. At least it wasn't just me. But would every class be like this?

Ms Ellergren stood in front of us with her arms folded. Er – had we done that badly?

'In case you hadn't worked it out,' she said, 'that was a test. Nobody groaned, no one complained. That is what I want to see. Excellence in all things, including endurance and doing exactly what you are told. Well done. I will see you on Thursday.'

We dragged ourselves to the changing rooms in silence. Even Stephanie didn't have enough energy to sneer at anyone, and that was a relief. Outside, I found Orrin waiting.

'What are you doing here?' I said.

'First night of my cleaning job. Hope you haven't made a mess.'

'Just the floor covered in my blood,' I said. 'How will I get home?'

He pointed to the street. 'Dad's waiting for you. See ya.'

I gave him a tired wave and mooched over to the car, slid onto the seat and lay back against the headrest.

'Tough class?' said Dad.

'Yep. I think I'll go to football training with Orrin. I need to get in better shape.'

'Why don't you go running with him?' He started the engine and put the car into gear. 'He bought some second-hand weights today. We could all lift dumbbells together. Even Mum's going to have a go, she says.'

'Brilliant,' I groaned. Weights? I would have been lucky to lift a feather pillow right then. But in the darkness of the car, I smiled to myself. That class had been the hardest I'd ever had, but I'd survived it. When Ms Ellergren said *Excellent*, she meant it.

Weightlifting? Maybe I'd give it a try.

CHAPTER 19

Dad and I arrived home just after Mum and we found her in the kitchen, leaning against the bench, staring out the window.

'What's up?' Dad said. 'Did you go?'

'Go where?' I asked.

'I went to watch the netball semi-final at your school,' said Mum.

I was too tired to manage more than a feeble 'What for?'

A pot of something boiled over behind her and she turned it down before answering. 'I wanted to watch the team before I decided about the coaching job.'

I dropped onto a chair and put my head in my hands. I didn't want to hear her decision. If she was coaching Jade's team, I'd be welcomed back into Jade's group with big smiles. Fake smiles. I wanted to be on my own; the outsider.

'So what did you think?' said Dad. 'Have you got the time?'

'It's not that.' Mum put her hand under my chin and

lifted my head up. 'Don't panic, Brynna, I'm not going to do it.'

'Oh.' I couldn't think of anything else to say. My brain had gone on strike.

'Don't you want to know why?'

'Jade's too horrible?'

'No.' Mum laughed. 'She's a good player, but a bit scrappy. And aggro, like you said. It was the parents. Ugh. Not like it was in my day at all. Shouting, swearing, abusing the umpires. I couldn't believe it.'

'Kids' sports are getting a bad name for that kind of thing,' Dad said. 'Same problem with the footy. They can't get enough umpires now. People are sick of being yelled and sworn at.'

'So, how was your class?' said Mum.

'Amazing,' I said. 'And I'm worn out. In a good way.'

Dad winked at Mum. 'Brynnie's going to lift weights with you and Orrin.'

'Good idea!' She nodded.

A sharp *Brrrrrrr* made us all jump. The phone rang so rarely at our house that we weren't used to it. Mum answered. 'Hello, Tam! How's things?'

Dad and I glanced at each other and waited, listening.

'Good, good,' Mum said. 'Well, you do what Uncle Tony says. If he wants you to work on Saturday, then you have to – it was your decision, Tam. And now it's your responsibility – no, we don't. Here, you can talk to Dad.'

She handed the phone over and Dad took it into the

lounge room. Through the closed door I could hear his voice rumbling. 'Tam's not in trouble up there, too, is he?'

Mum's mouth tightened as she turned the electric frypan on. 'No, but he will be if he doesn't stick to the agreement with Tony.' She began cracking eggs into a bowl. 'Grab the broccoli out of the fridge for me, Brynna. He's supposed to work two nights and Saturday mornings at the garage to pay his board, and now he wants to spend Saturdays with old Teddy Allen, learning blacksmithing.'

I held the sharp knife carefully, slicing broccoli and putting it into a pot. My heart felt heavy, but I knew better than to say anything. Mum's humming meant that she was busy thinking. Dad came back a couple of minutes later and hung up. All he said was, 'He'll learn one day. And it'll be the hard way, as usual.'

Mum made a funny snorting sound. 'I'd rather he was here with us, where we can keep an eye on him.'

'Don't worry. I had a quick word with Tony. He'll sort it out.'

'That's not Tony's job!' Mum said. 'He's our son.'

Dad put his arm around Mum's shoulders and squeezed. 'I reckon Tony will have a better chance of getting through to Tam than us right now.'

The back door opened and Orrin burst in, bringing cold air and stinky sweat with him. 'Dinner ready?' he said.

Mum sniffed and wrinkled her nose. 'Not until you've had a shower and a darned good scrub.'

'How was your training session?' said Dad.

'Full on! But I'll have to get stuck into those weights and some more running.'

Dad grinned at me. 'You two can train together.'

'Me train with the tiddler?' Orrin spluttered. 'No way.'

'Ha. You couldn't keep up with me,' I said.

As we all joked and talked, a small glow began to spread out inside me. Was it the class? Or my family, laughing in the kitchen? It didn't matter. For the first time in ages, I felt truly peaceful and ready to face the world.

The next few days rushed past – practice in the hall with Ricky, another rigorous class on Thursday night and Saturday class, then watching Orrin play and win Best on Field. I was so proud of him that I clapped until my hands stung.

Then we were into the last week of the school term. The netball final was Tuesday afternoon, and all classes were allowed to go and watch. It was being played at the high school gym nearby. I'd heard that our principal had stepped in to coach our team. He didn't know much about the game, but his wife was helping. Jade, Taylor and Lucy ignored me completely and I ate my lunch with Lala, the Sudanese girl. She was new, like me, and her English wasn't much good, so I was helping her. It was fun and way better than sitting alone.

We walked across to the high school together and sat up in the top row of seats, the bleachers. The gym seemed huge to me and I imagined being able to practise in here, pirouetting around and around. Even Ricky would've been able to jump and pirouette as much as he wanted.

And as if I'd conjured him up by thinking about him, there he was! Two other boys, all in the same uniform, had ambled into the gym with him and they stood there, looking around, nudging each other and slouching in that way boys did when they were trying to look cool. I grinned and said to Lala, 'Do Sudanese boys act like that?'

She rolled her eyes. 'Oh yes – only worse.'

Our team had been huddled in a group, talking with the principal, probably getting last-minute instructions, like the opposing team on the other side of the gym. I watched Jade, who was flicking back her hair and smoothing down her shirt at the same time as she checked round to see who was watching. She zeroed in on Ricky, who'd just sat down in the second row, and she straightened up. As soon as the principal finished talking, she strolled over in Ricky's direction.

It was obvious she knew all the boys and she stood there, hands on hips, chatting and tossing her head. Two of the boys laughed, but Ricky turned several times, as if he was more interested in finding someone in the crowd. Then he looked straight up at me, grinned and pointed his finger. I waved back and my face and neck felt hot. Jade's eyes followed Ricky's and when she saw me, her face tightened into its usual sullen mask. I grinned broadly and waved at her, too. So she turned her back and flounced off.

If I hadn't been at the top of her Most Hated List before, I sure was now.

'Who is that boy?' Lala said.

'Just a friend,' I said. I didn't want to explain the ballet thing.

'He *likes* you,' she said, giggling, and my face flamed all over again.

The game started and I followed it closely. Despite all her boasting, I'd never seen Jade play before, not even in training, and I was also keen to see how Lucy went. It soon became clear how our team operated. Jade was the centre, she hogged the ball ninety per cent of the time, and the only other girls who got their hands on it much were the goal shooters. Luckily, Jade was a terrific player. She also got penalised several times for shoving and grabbing the ball from opposing players, but never enough to warrant being sent off. Well, it was only a primary school championship.

Our two goal shooters were clearly nervous and missed lots of attempts. Still, at half-time we were ahead by two. During the break, Ricky decided to climb up to the top row and say hello. Of course, Lala giggled.

'What are you doing here?' I said. 'Shouldn't you be in class?'

'Nah. Our teacher's away sick, so the fill-in guy said we could come and watch.'

I couldn't resist it. 'Do you know Jade, from our team?'

'Who? Oh, her. Yeah,' he scoffed. 'She lives in my

street.' He pointed to a woman sitting in the front row, centre, with frizzy blonde hair. From here, we could see black roots and the glint of big gold earrings as they swayed from her ears. 'That's her mum. Being very, very quiet today. Usually she screams and shouts. Must've had a warning, hey?'

'Maybe she's the reason my mum didn't take on the coaching job,' I said.

'Is she a netball coach?' asked Lala.

'No – basketball.' I debated briefly with myself about whether I should say more. 'I told her she should coach you.'

Ricky's eyebrows shot up and his hands flexed like he was still holding his beloved ball. 'Me? I got no team.'

'You could find one,' I said. 'I keep telling you you're good.'

'No, you said I was good at –' He stopped himself in time, but his face was flushed.

'Good at what?' Lala asked. She nudged me and giggled. 'I *told* you.'

'*She*'s good at getting me into trouble,' Ricky said, pointing at me. 'Gotta go. See ya.'

He clambered back down to his seat and didn't look at me again. Luckily, the whistle went for the second half and I could ignore Lala's laughing eyes. The rest of the game was much like the first half and, with two minutes to go, the score was tied. Even I was sitting on the edge of my seat, cheering, and when Lucy grabbed the ball and threw it to our goal shooter, who put it through the hoop with ten seconds left, we all leapt up and cheered even louder.

'Did we win?' yelled Lala.

'Yes!' The big silver cup with blue ribbons tied to its handles was going to make Jade happy. As captain, she accepted it at the prize-giving afterwards, along with a medal for Player of the Match. For once, she laughed with joy. But as we lined up, ready to walk back to school, I saw Jade's mum talking to a man in a tracksuit and then grabbing Jade by the arm and dragging her over to talk to him, too. Jade was smiling, but it was her old fake smile again.

We didn't see her for the rest of the day and, with ballet class that night, I forgot about netball. But on Wednesday morning I found out all about it. The man was the selector for the state Under-14 netball team and Jade had been picked for the selection trials. She was so excited that even I was included in the circle around her, listening to her babble on about what the man said and admiring her medal.

At the youth hall that afternoon, Ricky helped me with the tables and copied everything I did, but he wasn't very talkative.

'Are you okay?' I said. 'If you're sick of dancing with me, you don't have to, you know.'

'No, it's fine,' he said. 'Keeps me fit. You're looking stronger, too.'

'I hope so. I've got classes three days a week, plus three afternoons here with you, and now everyone in our family is lifting weights and running. Well, me and Mum don't run; we walk fast.' Orrin left us all way behind, but it was fun working out with them. More fun than I'd expected.

'Cool.' That was all he said and, once we'd put the tables back, he said goodbye and left. I walked home alone in the thick, gloomy dusk, wondering if I'd upset him yesterday at the game. Surely he would've said. Fog was rolling in across the park and I shivered, sped up to jogging pace and got back to a warm, lit-up house. Mum was in the lounge room, lifting her legs up and down with small weight belts attached to them.

She passed me the local newspaper, folded open to the sports page. 'Is that your friend's team?'

Who – Jade? I read the small ad in the corner. *Coach wanted for Under-16 basketball team*. She must mean Ricky. 'I don't know. He said he didn't have a team anymore.'

'I've rung that number,' she said, puffing slightly. 'It sounds like his team – didn't you say their venue burnt down? That's what the man on the phone said.'

'You rang up?'

'Why not? I'm still interested in doing something like that, if they have crowd control for the parents. The high school has agreed finally to let them use the gym there.'

'Good. I think.' Was that why Ricky was so quiet? He was going to dump me and go back to basketball?

CHAPTER 20

Only six classes to go before the NBS audition, but who was counting? Me. Nobody dared to complain or groan in front of Ms Ellergren, but grumbles in the changing room were growing. There was no dancing in the intensive classes at all, only going over and over the same stuff on positions and steps and jetés and everything we all knew backwards. But Ms Ellergren seemed obsessed with absolute perfection, and we all felt more and more like an army regiment in every class.

It didn't bother me as much as the others – I knew I still had a lot of work to do on my arms. Ms Ellergren reprimanded me about it at least three times each class, and I'd had nightmares about it, too. Besides, I had my practice in the youth hall with Ricky, where we danced and created our own choreography and had fun. Even doing weights with Mum was fun, too. But the strain was showing on the other girls, especially Stephanie and Danielle.

I'd put my shoes on and was ready to go into the studio to warm up when they turned up, their whiny voices announcing them before they pushed open the changing room door. 'It's totally boring,' Stephanie said. 'She can't tell me the NBS is like this. I've been to the public days – they do all kinds of dancing.'

'My legs ache so much I can't get to sleep,' moaned Danielle.

Stephanie sniffed when she saw me. 'I suppose Miss Perfect here loves the boredom. Too dumb to manage anything more.'

'There's no dancing in the NBS audition,' I said. 'It's like a class. We've got to show we know the groundwork.'

'Oohh, groundwork. Where did you learn that big word?' Stephanie flipped her fingers at me.

I could hear Mum saying, *She's not worth wasting your time on*, so I scooted round to the door and left them sniggering behind me. In the studio, it took me a few minutes to calm down. My hands kept clenching, wanting to punch Stephanie in the face, and my legs felt jerky. I had to calm down, breathe. When class began, I'd settled down enough to concentrate, although I could still feel the anger seething away inside me and it actually energised me more. Several times, Ms Ellergren commended me on a jeté or an arabesque, and even my pirouettes earned me a smile.

But for every good mark she gave me, Stephanie's face darkened a bit more, and I dreaded facing her after class. As soon as we'd finished, I headed for the door, but Ms Ellergren called me back. 'Go and change,' she said, 'and then I want to talk to you.'

Stephanie had hung back to listen and now she glared at me and stalked away. In the changing room, she'd obviously said something nasty just before I walked in – I was greeted by silence, and Antoinette and Kate wouldn't look at me. I changed quickly, packed my bag and tucked it under the bench before returning to the studio. What did Ms Ellergren want? Was it me? Wasn't I doing well enough? Or wasn't Orrin cleaning the studio properly?

Ms Ellergren was reading some papers, which she put down on the piano before smiling at me. Two smiles in one day! 'I have been given the schedule for the NBS auditions,' she said. 'Your appointment is on the final day, Friday.'

'I'll tell Mum,' I said.

'You'll get a letter yourself, but you also need to give your mother these.' She handed me the papers. 'This is information about scholarships and bursaries. After watching you for the past few weeks, I have a very strong feeling that you will be selected, my dear.'

'Really?' I gulped and coughed. I was so astonished I could hardly speak.

She smiled again. 'Yes, really. But it's not just about your dancing. Has anyone explained about the physical analysis?'

I nodded. 'Mrs Calzotti said they examine your body and test things like your hip rotation and flexibility, and your Achilles tendons.'

'Exactly. That is a huge part of it. If your body isn't made for the extremely high level of dance expertise required, there's no point in their accepting you.' She held out her hand. 'Give me your foot.' I did as she asked and she told me to arch and flex it a few times while she held and stretched it more. 'Good. Now –' She let me stand again and gazed at me thoughtfully.

'Is there something wrong?'

Why was I here? Despite everything, was she about to tell me I was wasting my time?

'A ballet dancer needs more than the right body and perfection in the basics. What I see in you, Brynna, is the artist with a soul, but it needs more nurturing. Do you practise outside class time?'

'Yes, of course.'

'Your technique is very good now – I can see you've been working hard. What I want you to concentrate on is the poetry and music in your dancing. Save technique for this class. Explore yourself through experimenting and dancing. Use *Swan Lake* or one of the other ballets, play the music and feel your way into responding to it.' She tilted her head. 'That's all. See you on Saturday.'

I left the studio, a bit dazed, her words whirling through my head. The changing room was empty and I barely noticed that my bag was on top of the bench instead of under it. Mum was waiting outside for me. As we drove home, I chatted to her, but my brain was on another planet. It wasn't until I unpacked my bag in my bedroom that I realised something was wrong with my ballet shoes. The ribbons were missing, but it was more than that. I held them up in horror. Someone had cut big holes in them, holes that would be impossible to repair.

'Mum!'

My scream held all my dismay and hurt and panic. She came running. 'What? Are you hurt? Did you fall?'

With the tears rolling down my face, I showed her my shoes. 'They're ruined!'

Her mouth simply gaped. She stared at the shoes as if she couldn't believe what she was seeing. 'Who on earth did that?'

'Stephanie.' Who else would be so vindictive?

She grabbed them from me. 'Right,' she said grimly. 'What's this girl's surname? I need to have a few words with her mother.'

Mum angry wasn't something you wanted to experience, and one part of me loved the idea of her paying out on Stephanie and her mother, but another part said Stop. 'There's no point. It'll only make her happy that she's upset me.'

'I can't let this go, Brynna. I did it once before and it messed things up for years.'

'What do you mean? What happened?' Here it was, the secret again, the extra thing she'd never told me. Was she going to tell me now?

She sat heavily on my bed, gripping my shoes as if they were stress balls. 'The Olympic team. Why I never went to Seoul.'

'You were injured,' I said. 'Of course you'd be upset about it.'

She shook her head. 'It was more than that. The accident on the court – it wasn't an accident. The other girl didn't trip and fall on my leg. She did it on purpose. She saw I'd landed awkwardly with my leg out and she pretended to trip.'

I stared at Mum and my heart stopped for a moment, then banged in my chest so loudly that it gave me a fright. I gasped. 'Did they ban her? Did she get penalised?'

'No,' she snorted. 'She was all over me with apologies and they believed her.'

'How could she live with it?' I said. 'She stopped you from competing in the Olympics!'

'She lived with it just fine. She went to the trials and made the team.'

Finally I understood what Mum was talking about – that some people would do anything to get what they wanted. A deep, dark chill ran through me. 'Are you saying that Stephanie might do something like that to me? If we don't tell her mum?'

'Yes. This has to stop now, before she does worse. I have no doubt her mother will deny it – she might even be spurring her on – but by speaking out, we let them know we'll fight back.'

'Did you fight back?' I asked her, hoping she wouldn't be mad with me.

'No.' Mum held up my ruined shoes. 'I didn't want to look like I was sour-graping. But instead it ate away at me for years and destroyed my love of the game. If I'd said something then, made an official complaint – because I did have supporters who agreed with me – then at least I would've dealt with it, instead of shoving it aside.'

I looked at the ruined shoes. They were nothing compared to a broken leg. 'But you did keep playing.'

'Not really. The woman moved to Bendigo and I couldn't bear to be on the same court as her. I chickened out. Stupid me.'

I'd never heard Mum talk like this before, but now I began to understand all the things she'd said to me, what lay behind them. More than ever, I didn't want to let her down. 'Okay, let's do it.'

Needless to say, Stephanie's mum was abusive on the phone, denied it all and said I was just jealous of Stephanie. But Mum had the last word. 'I'll be keeping these shoes as evidence. If I see any more of this kind of behaviour directed at Brynna, I'll make damn sure your daughter is expelled from Ms Ellergren's school. You can bet on it!' And she slammed down the phone.

'There,' she said to me. 'Done.'

I hugged her again, and knew that somehow Mum had just blasted a demon of her own into outer space.

CHAPTER 21

I was half-expecting Ricky not to turn up at the youth hall the following afternoon, but he was there and full of energy with his basketball tucked under his arm.

'You want to dance or shoot hoops?' I said.

'Dance! Basketball's tomorrow night.'

'You mean your old team's back together?'

'Not really,' he said. 'This'll be a new team and the rumour is that we're getting a new coach. I didn't think anyone would want to coach a team from round here.'

I hesitated. Mum hadn't actually said she was applying for the job. Besides, if she did get the coaching gig, she mightn't want me saying who she was. It felt weird, seeing her become this person who was an expert in something other than being Mum, but I didn't want to mess it up for her. 'So, are we dancing or not?'

'Yeah.' He looked sheepish.

'What's the matter?'

'I brought some music.' He pulled a mess of cords and little boxes out of the front of his jacket. 'See? iPod and speakers.'

'Those tiny things will be loud enough?'

'Sure. Wait and see.'

'Okay. Let's warm up first.' What kind of music did he think we were going to dance to? Rap? Hip-hop? He'd have a good laugh at me when he discovered I had no idea how to dance to those things. I'd have to wait and see what it was.

Having to force my feet into my old shoes was horrible, but they were all I had. Luckily I hadn't grown any more, so it was the familiar pinching I was used to. I sighed and tied my ribbons, trying not to think about my damaged shoes. We went through all the barre and centre exercises, then he set up the little iPod unit and pressed *Play*. I nearly fell over when *Swan Lake* burst out of the speakers.

'Where did you get that from?'

He grinned. 'Off the internet.'

'It's my favourite!'

'Cool. So, what'll we do?' He stood there, waiting for me to lead the way. I'd watched the ballet on video lots of times and knew the story and what each dance was about – I'd even pretended to dance some of them myself, in front of the TV, when no one else was home.

'I'll dance what I can,' I said, 'and maybe you follow me. But a lot of the real ballet is on pointe, which I can't do.'

He nodded and waited, watching me position myself at the side of the room. I felt so stupid, trying to be a ballerina in *Swan Lake*, of all things! But Ricky was totally serious about giving it a go, and I remembered what Ms Ellergren had said. It didn't matter if the steps were the same as I'd seen – all I had to do was let the music take me. After a few minutes, I watched him and realised that's what he was doing. He'd given up copying, and was just dancing whatever he felt like. There wasn't much ballet in it, but his rhythm and grace left me gobsmacked. If I could capture some of that, Ms Ellergren would be smiling, for sure.

Ricky stopped at the end of the room. 'Aren't we supposed to dance together?' he said, puffing. 'You know, you do those turn things and I hold your arm and stuff?'

'A lot of it is the male and female together, only there are two different girls in it. It takes a long time to learn to dance together like that.' I sat down to rest, too, for a few moments. 'You usually have a choreographer, who shows you what the steps are and how to put it all together.'

'Why are there two different girls?'

'Do you know the story?' He shook his head. 'Odette is the main ballerina. In the story, she's got a curse on her, so in the daytime she's a swan and at night she turns back into a woman again. This prince comes along and falls in love with her, but he can't break the curse until he declares his love and the sorcerer stops him. Then the sorcerer makes up a fake Odette called Odille, and sends her along to trick the prince.'

'Whoa, I can see this is not going to end happily.'

'You're right – it doesn't. The prince announces his marriage to the wrong one, Odille, and then because the curse can't be broken, the prince and Odette both drown themselves in the lake.' I laughed at his expression. 'Don't be too sad. It's a beautiful ballet, my favourite.'

'The music is all orchestra – doesn't anyone ever sing?'

'No. There are some really good bits, though.' Just then, the music changed to the next part and I leapt up. 'This is the "Dance of the Little Swans". It's really famous.'

'Because?'

'Watch.' I got into position and started dancing along to the familiar music. I kept my feet moving and my hands crossed as if I were dancing in a quartet. 'This is four cygnets dancing together, with their hands joined, but there's only one of me.' After a couple of minutes, my feet couldn't keep up and I stopped.

'That is a seriously weird dance,' said Ricky.

I folded my arms. 'You really should come to dance class with me, you know.'

'Nah, don't be silly. I'm just having a bit of fun, that's all.' He pointed at his watch. 'Time's up. I've got to go and shoot some hoops, get my eye in for tomorrow night.'

'You're really excited about the team, aren't you?'

'Yeah, but don't tell anyone.' He pulled at his ear. 'And I'll still come and help you with the tables, don't worry.'

'What about the dancing?' I tried to keep my face blank, like I didn't care either way, but I could feel my mouth drooping.

'That, too. This *bell-ay* stuff is helping me get fit to play.'

He waved his arms around, to pretend he was kidding, but I knew he was at least a little bit hooked on dancing! Maybe one day I could convince him to take a class or two.

When I arrived home after practice at the youth hall, Mum was on the phone, pacing up and down the hallway, waving her free arm around. 'Yes, not a problem. We'll see. Could be two or three, could be swamped. Okay, thanks. Thanks a million. Bye.'

She pressed the *Off* button and shouted, 'Woohoooo!' Then she grabbed my shoulder and laughed. 'I'm doing it, Brynnie. Coaching the team. How good's that?' She sobered up. 'Of course, I need a team to coach. I mightn't get enough turning up. But I'm sure we could advertise.'

'Well, you'll have one very keen player, that's for sure,' I said. 'Ricky's busting to play. He'll be the whole team if you want.'

'This is your friend who's at the youth hall?'

'Yep. He's a great player.'

'Really?' Mum peered at me. 'Or are you just saying that because he's your friend?'

'No way. You'll see.'

'Excellent. One down; eight or nine to go.' She strode into the kitchen, left the phone on the table and checked the pots on the stove, then paced into the lounge and back again. 'I'll need to keep up my exercises, maybe see the physio about some harder ones. I want to make sure my leg's a hundred per cent.'

I hated to break into her excitement, but it was important. 'Mum, can I – can we –' I swallowed hard. 'Mum, I need new ballet shoes. I'm sorry it'll cost more money, but with the extra classes, and the audition getting close –'

She stopped pacing immediately. 'It's all right; it wasn't your fault. I've already squeezed the budget and your dad got some overtime tonight.' She kissed the top of my head. 'You can go tomorrow on your own, can't you? To buy them?'

Now I was happy enough to dance a jig, maybe even try some of Ricky's rap. No, on second thoughts, I'd prefer the cygnets' dance! 'Absolutely,' I said.

The rest of the school holidays went in a whirl of practice with Ricky, classes, running with Mum and Orrin, and watching Mum become as mad about basketball as I was about ballet.

I tried hard not to think about the NBS audition too much, because whenever I did, my heart sped up and my hands got sweaty and I'd find I was gritting my teeth. One practice session at a time, I kept telling myself. Make this one count, make it your best ever. But then I'd lie in bed at night and the steps and positions would flick through my mind like a crazy movie until I wanted to bang my head against the wall.

Every night at the dinner table, Mum either babbled

on and on about 'her team' or sat staring into space. She said she was running through plays in her head. Dad and Orrin and I learnt to ignore her, but we'd all promised to go to the first game, the day after my audition. All she said to me about Ricky was, 'Talented, but undisciplined.' I wasn't sure whether she meant he had real potential or not.

Ricky still came to the youth hall and helped me with the tables, but then he started saying, 'I have to train, sorry. Need to work on my ball skills, or Coach will put me on the bench.' And he'd climb back out of the window and race off to the basketball court. Once I nearly said to him, 'You know, your coach is my mum.' But somehow the words never made it out of my mouth. Mum would treat him exactly like the other players, because she didn't believe in favourites and Ricky didn't really need to know.

But I missed dancing with him. On the days when he left me to practise alone, it seemed so much harder to stick to my routine, let alone feel inspired and flowing when I danced. With one week to go before the big day, my legs and arms were heavy logs, my posture stiff, and even *Swan Lake* couldn't lift my spirits.

The audition was going to be a huge disaster, I just knew it. I decided I had to tell Mum that I'd pull out and not waste everyone's time, but she was buzzing around, drawing plays on an old whiteboard in the lounge, humming to herself. I didn't want to bother her. And no one else would have understood. I sure couldn't talk to Ms Ellergren about it – she'd think I was a total failure!

At each class, Stephanie and Danielle acted like I had the plague and smirked whenever Ms Ellergren reprimanded me. Even David, Antoinette and Kate hardly talked to me, although I thought that was because they were feeling like me – overwhelmed and depressed. I was the only one who had a Friday audition; everyone else's was on Thursday, and nobody mentioned them, as if it might cause a jinx.

It was a relief when school started again. Lucy had been away during the holidays and missed Saturday classes and when she saw me, she said, 'Hey, why the long face? Did you miss me?'

I nearly burst into tears and bit the inside of my mouth so hard I could taste blood. I bent down quickly and pretended to be looking for something in my bag until I felt able to talk without my voice wobbling. 'Where did you go for your holiday?' I asked.

'The Gold Coast. The theme parks were awesome,' she said, bouncing up and down. 'You should see my photos of the tigers and me and Mum on the roller-coaster. I screamed so much, I nearly died.'

I forced a big smile. 'Sounds fantastic. I can't imagine my mum on a roller-coaster.'

'Mum said she wanted to cheer me up.' She shrugged. 'To be honest, I'd rather have been in class with you.'

'Not with Stephanie and Danielle, though,' I said. 'They've been hideous.'

'Hassling you? Or worse?'

I told her about my shoes. 'What?' Her mouth dropped open. 'Did you tell Ms Ellergren?'

'No, Mum yelled at Stephanie's mother and Stephanie hasn't done anything else. Except give me the usual nasty comments and looks.'

Jade loomed up behind Lucy. 'Hey, girlfriend, where's your tan?'

'Girlfriend'? What TV show was she watching now? Within a couple of minutes, Jade was trying to drag Lucy away, leaving me on my own, but for once Lucy resisted. We walked into class together and I began to feel a bit more cheerful. I mightn't be able to explain to Lucy about how depressed I was about the audition, but at least I could tell her about Stephanie and have a laugh.

For the first time, when I got to the youth hall at four, Ricky wasn't at the window. I waited for more than ten minutes and then I had to ask one of the boys watching TV to help me with the tables. Why now? I fumed, tying my ribbons and pulling my sweatshirt off with jerky hands. Why would he let me down this week? I went through the barre and centre exercises like a robot, and then realised that with Ricky not there, I had no music. Give up, a little voice nagged me. Give up, what's the use?

'No, I won't give up,' I said aloud. 'I won't be a quitter, even if everyone else is!'

I went to the side of the room and stood for a few moments, eyes closed, breathing, trying to quell the churning and twisting inside of me. I visualised rough waves at the beach, a sunny day, the waves calming down, smoothing out, while I breathed and tried to relax the tensed-up muscles in my shoulders and neck. I could do it. I could be a swan, gliding across the water.

When my body finally felt almost normal again, instead of made of fractured rocks, I opened my eyes. Pirouettes. There was a silver cord, lifting me up, a shining line from head to toe. Away I went – one, two, three, four, five. And again. Five more and back again. Not one wobble, one falter, one misstep. Quiet happiness bloomed inside me and I smiled the whole time I was changing shoes and getting help with the tables – I even smiled the whole way home, knowing I'd sleep that night with perfect pirouettes in my dreams.

CHAPTER 22

Our house was in darkness; there were no cars in the driveway. When I let myself in, the doorhandle seemed icy, the air inside thick and stale. I turned the kitchen light on and made myself some hot chocolate, then peeled potatoes for dinner. Still there was no one home. Maybe Orrin was out running, but where was Mum? Or Dad?

The phone rang, jarring the silence, and I dropped the knife into the sink in fright.

'Hello?'

'Brynna, you're home. Thank goodness.'

'Mum? Where are you?'

'I'm at –' She took a deep breath and the sound of it chilled me down to my bones. 'I'm at the hospital. Your dad's had an accident at work.'

'What?' I was sure I'd heard her wrong. 'What do you mean, "accident"? What happened?'

'Never mind that now,' she said. 'Orrin will be home shortly and he'll bring you back.'

'Orrin can't drive.' I seemed to be saying stupid things,

but I couldn't help it. What did she mean by 'accident'? 'Is Dad all right?'

'They won't tell me anything yet. He's still in the operating theatre.'

'But –'

'Look, I haven't got time to discuss it. Just wait for Orrin, all right?' Her voice was high-pitched, like she was hanging on by her fingernails.

She hung up in my ear and I put the phone down gently. My whole body felt like it was made of cotton wool and I had to sit down. My head spun – what had happened? Was Dad going to die? Why wouldn't she tell me?

I hadn't even known I was crying, but now I couldn't stop. I grabbed a handful of tissues and jammed them into my eyes, held my breath and tried to stop being such a wuss. Mum wouldn't want me to bawl like a little kid and I didn't want Orrin to see me in a mess either. The tears gradually stopped and I washed my face in cold water.

A car horn tooted outside and, a few seconds later, Orrin burst in the back door. 'Come on,' he said, 'the taxi's waiting.'

'Taxi'? I'd been in a taxi maybe once in my whole life. I scrambled out the door behind him and got into the back seat.

'Back to Western General, mate, thanks,' Orrin said, and the taxi roared off down the street.

'What's happened to Dad?' I said.

'Didn't Mum tell you?'

'No.'

'He got hit by a forklift. Actually, he got hit by the load of pipes on the forklift.' He rubbed his hands over his face. 'The guy wasn't watching where he was going – he had the load on wrong. It fell off and Dad and another guy got crushed.'

'That's terrible! Is he going to be okay?'

'Um –' His mouth trembled and a stab of fear went through my stomach. I held on so tight to the door handle, I nearly pulled it off the door. 'The other guy's dead. Dad's being operated on. They said he's critical and they can't tell us anything yet.'

I couldn't speak. How could this have happened to my dad?

The hospital was quiet inside, with nurses bustling along on soft-soled shoes and murmuring to each other. We went up in a huge lift, Orrin leaning against the wall with his arms wrapped around himself. When the doors slid open, he pointed to the left and I followed him down a corridor with a shiny floor. Was Dad back in a room already? No. Around the next corner there was a waiting area with dingy lounge chairs and a couple of low tables piled with tattered magazines. Mum sat in the far corner, staring out of the darkened window at lights in the distance.

As we got nearer, she looked around and saw me, and held out her arms. I rushed to sit next to her and she hugged me tightly. 'Brynnie, you're here.'

'What's happening? Have they operated on Dad yet?'

'He's still in there. We have to wait – and it could be long while.' She smiled at Orrin. 'Thanks, love.'

Orrin nodded and slouched in the next chair with his hands in his pockets.

My tummy rumbled loudly and Mum reached for her bag. 'You're right. It's dinner time and no one's eaten.'

'I'm not hungry,' Orrin said.

'Me neither.' My stomach said it was hungry, but it also said it was so churned up that eating might not be a good idea.

'You both need to eat and I do too. If I drink any more coffee, my eyes will pop out.' She gave Orrin a twenty-dollar note. 'Take Brynna down to the café and find us all some food that isn't too terrible, will you?'

He took the money and I followed him again, feeling like a sheep. We found the café on a lower floor and stood in front of the packets of dry-looking sandwiches and cakes. 'It's this, or those pies and sausage rolls,' he said.

The pies looked like they'd been in the heater for days. 'Isn't there anything else?'

'I guess it's sandwiches then.' We picked the ones that looked edible, bought cold drinks as well and carried them back upstairs. Mum said maybe we shouldn't be eating in the waiting area, but no one else was around to tell us off, so we went ahead. My cheese and ham sandwich was like cardboard, but nothing would have tasted any different. And at least the orange juice was cold.

The hours dragged on. We all took turns pacing. We

stopped to read the noticeboards and stare out the windows, then sat down again. There was nothing to talk about that made any sense, not while we were sitting there waiting to find out whether Dad was going to live or die. Every time I thought about it, my eyes burned and I had to blink hard, over and over, to stop the tears.

By eleven o'clock, both Orrin and I were lying across the lounge chairs, dozing. I'd keep hearing footsteps and jerk up to see who it was, but it was usually a nurse in the corridor. A couple of times a nurse in a different uniform came and told us there was no news yet, and each time Mum said thanks and we all went back to waiting.

Just before midnight, we heard doors opening and closing and footsteps in the corridor. We all sat up as a man in pale blue scrubs, his face tired and lined, came into the waiting area.

'Mrs Davies?'

'Yes?' Mum jumped up, but then she froze, like she couldn't get her feet to move any closer to him. I couldn't move either – I could hardly breathe. Had this doctor come to tell us Dad was dead?

The doctor rubbed his face with both hands as he faced Mum. 'Your husband's out of theatre and so far he's holding his own. We'll have to keep a very close eye on him now. His head injury was the most serious and immediate thing to deal with. They'll be taking him up to intensive care in a little while.'

'Right. Thanks,' Mum whispered.

'Have you got any questions?'

I knew the question we all wanted to ask – was Dad going to die? But no one was game to say it. Mum shook her head. 'No. Not at the moment.'

'Right, then.' He looked at us, then back to Mum again. 'If you go up to the intensive care ward in about twenty minutes, they'll let you see him for a few minutes.'

He left and Mum sank down into her seat again and burst into tears, scrabbling in her bag for tissues. Orrin and I gaped at her – Mum never cried. But something this bad had never happened to us before.

'Don't worry,' she said, taking a shuddering breath, 'I'll calm down in a minute. It's just all been a bit much.'

'You go for it, Mum,' Orrin said. 'I might even join you.'

'Are they going to let us in to see Dad?' I said. 'Or just you?'

'I don't know. We'll ask when we go up.'

We sat close together, watching the clock tick over the minutes. Twenty, nineteen, eighteen – the seconds were dragging and Orrin jumped up and paced round the room, his arms folded, shoulders hunched. It was as if he had so much energy pent up inside that he couldn't stay still. Then he dropped to the floor and started doing push-ups. Mum and I couldn't believe it, but we said nothing. I wanted to join him, but instead I sat, jiggling my legs and watching the clock again.

'Twenty minutes is up,' Orrin said.

It was only seventeen, but we leapt up and rushed

towards the lift together. He jabbed at the button for the fifth floor and we stood there in silence. When the lift doors opened, it felt like slow motion as we stepped out and walked over to the nurses' station. Mum asked about Dad and a nurse pointed to a room two doors down. 'Only for two minutes,' she said.

I wasn't sure what to expect. Would Dad be all covered in bandages? Would he look like Dad? Maybe he'd be hooked up to a dozen machines and look like a machine himself. But when we were finally allowed into his room, he was still unconscious. I was right about the machines and they beeped and flashed continuously, but I guessed that meant he was alive and doing everything he was supposed to – like breathe and have a heartbeat.

Mum was almost too scared to touch him. She laid her hand over his – the one that didn't have a tube going into it – and took a deep breath. Orrin and I stood near the end of the bed.

The bandage around Dad's head was the worst bit. It made him look like a mummy, as if he was already dead, and his face was pale and a bit whiskery. After what seemed like only about ten seconds, the nurse said we had to leave. 'You could go home now, if you like,' she said. 'He'll be unconscious for some time yet.'

'Where's the waiting room here?' was all Mum said and when the nurse showed us to a room at the end of the corridor, we filed in and sat down again. Mum went to the toilet and came back with her face damp and her eyes shadowed. 'I think you two should go home and get some sleep. I'll stay with your dad, just in case – he wakes up.'

'I'm not going home,' said Orrin.

'Me neither,' I added.

Mum hugged us both. 'Better get comfortable on these chairs then.' She took out her mobile phone. 'It's very late, but I think I'd better ring Tony and let him know what's happening.'

From Mum's end of the call, I worked out that she'd already rung Uncle Tony earlier, and that he and Aunty Sue and Tam were still up, waiting to hear from her.

'Yes, if you want to come down, that would be great, Tony,' said Mum. 'Yes, bring Tam, please.' She talked to Tam for a couple of minutes, telling him about Dad, and then said goodbye and pressed the *Off* button, sighing. 'I feel better now. They'll be here by eight in the morning, he said. I did want him to bring Tam, more than anything.'

I hadn't even thought about Tam! My brain had been focused on the hospital and Dad, and watching that long corridor, waiting for someone to come and tell us the news. What would Tam say? Would he want to come back to Melbourne now because of Dad? It seemed like he'd been gone for months, but it was only a few weeks. I wondered what it had been like for him, going back to his old school. Mum had been calling him several times a week and once or twice I'd talked to him, but he wasn't into conversation much, so after a few grunts, I ended up handing the phone back to Mum.

Again, we sat in the uncomfortable chairs and stared

at the floor and ceiling, and Mum leafed through another pile of old magazines. 'Are you going to stay awake all night, Mum?' I said.

'No, I'll try and sleep soon, even though these chairs will probably cripple me for life. Why don't you lie down? You'll fit on them better than either of us.'

'Okay.' I stretched out across three chairs, trying to ignore the gaps and the bits digging into me. Everything was quiet, except for the hum of airconditioning and faint beeping sounds from the rooms. My eyes closed and I slept, but the chairs and Mum and Orrin talking kept waking me up, then I dipped into black depths and didn't hear another thing.

My dreams were all jumbled up, with Ricky and Ms Ellergren dancing around me, and Mimi playing the piano. Lucy and Jade were reading a huge book with pictures in it that they wouldn't show me, then suddenly I was in a hospital bed like Dad, with my whole body wrapped in bandages so I couldn't move. I knew that I wanted to dance, but a nurse kept pushing me back on the bed and Ms Ellergren stood by the door, watching a big clock. I couldn't see the time on it, because her head was in the way. Then she said, 'Too late, you're out,' and disappeared.

I woke with a start and waved my arms around wildly, feeling as if I was about to fall off the narrow chairs. The air conditioning had got colder and I had goosebumps all over me. What had that dream been about? An awful feeling of dread curdled in my stomach and I felt like my sandwich was about to come up again. The clock above the doorway read

3:45, and outside it was still pitch black. Nowhere near dawn. I needed to go to the toilet and stood up slowly, unbending all the kinks from my body.

Mum and Orrin were both asleep, with their heads back and mouths open. Orrin was snoring lightly and Mum looked really uncomfortable. I supposed they were both like me – so tired that they slept anyway. I wandered down the corridor and found the toilets at the other end. I was too wide awake now, so I washed my face and arms and drank some water, still thinking about the dream.

Then it hit me. It was Tuesday. Today was class day, the last one before we went for our auditions. A really important class, Ms Ellergren had said. There was no way I could go and I knew I wouldn't be going to school either. How could I, with Dad lying here, nearly dead? What would we do if he died? I looked at myself in the mirror and my face said it all. I looked like a ghoul, with big black holes for eyes and white skin. Even my mouth was white. A terrible ache grew in my throat and I wanted to cry but the tears wouldn't come. Instead the ache grew bigger until I thought it was going to choke me, or my chest was going to split open.

Oh Dad, please don't die, I begged, *please!* I couldn't imagine our lives without him. His big laugh, his capable hands fixing things for us, his arms hugging Mum, hugging me, the way he was always there when we needed something, his quiet voice that calmed me down, his faith in our talents, his hard work –

I ran out of the bathroom and down the corridor,

searching for his room. There – but the door was closed. I peered in through the glass but there was no one inside, just Dad, lying with his eyes closed and the machines blinking and beeping around him. The nurses must be with other people. I turned the handle as quietly as I could until it clicked, pushed the door open and slipped inside, closing it behind me.

The room smelled of laundry detergent and disinfectant, of strange medicinal smells and faint sweat. Dad seemed to be hardly breathing, but I could hear the gentle *whoosh* of his air machine, pushing air into him through a plastic thing in his nose. The big bag of clear stuff on the stand next to his bed dripped liquid into him through another tube taped to his arm. There was only one chair in the room, in a corner, and I lifted it over to his bed, sitting close enough so I could touch his hand. He was so still that if it wasn't for the air sound, I might've thought he was dead, but when I looked closely, I could see his chest rising just a tiny bit and relief rushed through me. He really was alive! And when I put my hands over his hand, it was warm and the hairs stuck up on it just like they always did.

I realised he wouldn't know I was there, but I felt a million times better being able to touch him and know that, so far, he was holding his own. I wanted to tell him lots of things, but if he couldn't hear me, what was the point? Somehow, it didn't seem to matter. Then again, maybe he *could* hear me. I'd read that people in comas could hear what was being said. So I knew I had to try.

CHAPTER 23

I kept holding Dad's hand and watched his still face for any sign that he knew I was there, beside him. 'Hi, Dad,' I whispered. 'It's me, Brynna. I just wanted to make sure you were all right. Mum's here and so's Orrin, and Tam's coming soon, too.'

Whoosh, whoosh, beep, beep.

Then it spilt out of me. 'I had a bad dream, Dad. I know you always said bad dreams don't mean anything, it's just your brain getting rid of rubbish, but this one was real. It had Ms Ellergren in it and she was really mad at me.' I swallowed hard. 'I'm not going to do the audition, Dad. I just can't, not now. I mean, I know I was feeling really down about it before and thinking I'd fail, but it's not that. Truly, it's not. I'm not a quitter – you know I'm not. But this is different. You're more important than anything. I'd give it all up so you'd get better. Not that I think giving up ballet would save your life or anything.'

Whoosh, beep, whoosh, beep.

'But that's our family, isn't it? We do stuff for each

other, like you and Mum moving down here so I could do ballet. And now this has happened and you're not going anywhere for a while, so I've got to help Mum now.' Tears rolled down my face and dripped onto the white cotton bedcover. I didn't want to let go of Dad's hand. 'I'll still keep going on Saturdays, because I think we can work that out and it won't matter if I miss a few, but I know the Ballet School isn't going to be possible now, and I can apply again next year. They'll understand.

'So don't you worry, Dad. We want you to get better, without worrying about stuff for us. We'll manage, but we need you to come back, Dad, we need you to be our dad. That's more important than anything. You promise?'

I wished that his hand would move, or that his eyes would open. I wished that he'd say, 'That's not a problem, Brynna, I'll be out of here today and it'll all be back to normal.' But I knew he couldn't.

I lay my head down on the bedcover, my hands still over his, and closed my eyes. I wasn't tired, I just wanted to stay there and rest a bit longer.

'Brynna. Brynna.' A hand shook my shoulder.

'Go away. It's not school today.' My brain slowly woke up and told me I wasn't in my bed at home and I jerked upright. 'What!'

Mum bent over me. 'How long have you been in here?'

'I dunno. What's the time?'

'It's after eight. Tam's here and your Uncle Tony.'

'Are they coming in to see Dad?' I asked. Dad! I glanced at the bed, but he still lay there, unmoving.

'They might be allowed in for a couple of minutes. Come on, the nurse wants us out of here. They need to do checks on your dad now.'

I followed her out and the nurse patted my shoulder. She didn't seem to mind that I'd been in there so long. In the waiting room, Tam and Uncle Tony stood by the window, their faces drawn with worry. Orrin sat in a lounge chair, drinking coffee from a paper cup and screwing up his nose at the taste. I hugged Tam and Uncle Tony and they both held on for a long time.

'Sitting with your dad, were you?' Uncle Tony said, sniffing.

'Yeah. But he's still unconscious.'

'What's the latest then?' he asked Mum.

'The same. They're waiting and watching. Either this afternoon or tomorrow, he'll have a CT scan on his brain. They said if something is happening in there, it'll take a day or two to show up.' She sighed. 'So far, it's a skull fracture. Hopefully, nothing else will go wrong inside his head.'

Uncle Tony winced. 'Should you be telling the kids this?'

'We all want to know exactly what's happening,' Orrin said. 'It's not knowing that sends you psycho.'

'What about the other injuries?' said Uncle Tony.

There were more?

'Broken arm, cracked ribs, a neck injury that they

can't do anything about right now apart from keeping him in one place and seeing how it goes.' Mum sat down suddenly as if her legs had given way. 'At least he's alive. That other poor man –'

My tummy gurgled so loudly that everyone heard it and swung around. My face burned, but Mum smiled. 'Life,' she said. 'You're right, Brynna. We've got to eat, breathe, do our best.'

'Sorry,' I said.

'It's breakfast time,' she said. 'Your tummy's just reminding you of what we'd forgotten. Being in this place is like living in another time zone. Tony, they said they'll let you and Tam in for a couple of minutes, but not yet. Why don't we go and get something to eat, and come back in a while.'

So we all piled into the lift and ate scrambled eggs and toast and coffee in the café downstairs. Even Tam was smiling a bit, once his stomach was full. When we went back up to the ICU, the others were allowed quick visits to Dad, but I stayed outside. I could see through the window that he was the same as before.

Mum decided we should go home and have showers and get changed, then she and Uncle Tony went back to the hospital for a couple of hours. Tam, Orrin and I tried to watch TV, but there was nothing on worth watching and we were sick of all our DVDs. Orrin went for a run and I thought about some ballet exercises, but I couldn't bring myself to even get my shoes out.

How would I let Ms Ellergren know I couldn't do the class? I could call her, but I couldn't think how to explain it in a way she'd understand. But if I went to the studio, I'd see the other girls and that'd make it so hard to pull out. It was after three and I had to decide what to do or it'd be too late for anything. Mum had rung from the hospital to say Dad wasn't having his scan till five o'clock, so she was staying until after it was done.

I rang Ms Ellergren's number, but no one answered and she didn't have voicemail – not that I would have left a message anyway. That would really have sounded like I didn't care. I had to go to the studio. If I talked to her early, I could get out of there before anyone arrived.

Orrin came in from his run, puffing and red-faced. I explained where I was going. 'Does Mum know?' he said.

'Where I'm going? No, I only decided just now.'

'No – does she know you're not doing the class?'

'I can't go to class with all this happening. Everything's changed.' I searched for my backpack. 'Have you got any money? I need a ticket for the bus.'

'But we organised everything so you could do this special class. You can't chuck it in. What about the audition?'

I couldn't bear to think about that. The class was hard enough. I stared at the label on my backpack until I'd forced the threatening tears away. 'Mum needs our help. We don't know what's going to happen with Dad. Even when he comes out of hospital, he won't be able to go back to work, not for ages.'

'But –' He looked around as if hoping Mum would materialise and stop me.

'There's no point going to the class and the audition isn't going to happen. Mum and Dad'll need the fee money they're going to save. Even with a bursary, we can't afford the Ballet School. We might even have to go back to Bendigo.' With my jaw set, I held out my hand. 'Money? Please?'

He sighed. 'I think you're making a big mistake. You should talk to Mum first.'

'I can't. The last class is tonight and I'll probably be back at the hospital, like you.' I took the five-dollar note he gave me. 'I couldn't dance properly anyway, not with Dad lying in that bed, all bandaged up.'

'Fine, then.' He held up his hands. 'But you can explain to Mum when she gets home.'

I didn't answer him. I couldn't. My throat ached and I wanted to get out of the house as fast as I could. Besides, I wasn't going to tell Mum anything. She had enough to worry about. I was taking one of the worries off her plate.

The bus dropped me in the street next to the studio and by the time I walked there, it was after four-thirty and the door was open. Hearing the faint tinkle of the piano, I slipped inside and gazed at all the ballet photos for a few minutes. One day that would be me, but not right now. I crossed the foyer and pulled open the studio door. Inside, Ms Ellergren was leaning over the piano, talking to Mimi.

'We'll start with that one, I think, and try the Mozart

second,' she said. As I approached, she turned and smiled. 'Brynna, you're nice and early.'

'Um – I'm not here for the class, Ms Ellergren.' Her smile flipped over into a frown and my feet faltered, then I kept moving and came to a stop in front of her. 'I can't do the class. I'm very sorry. I really wanted to but – my dad –' I swallowed hard and had to take a couple of breaths. 'Dad had an accident at work and Mum's at the hospital and I can't do the audition on Friday either. Things at home just aren't – right.'

'Are you sure?' Her voice was gentle. 'Tonight's class is not a problem. And your father might be much better by Friday.'

I shook my head. 'It's changed everything. It's the money, too, that's part of it, but if Dad – when Dad can come home, he'll need looking after and Mum can't do everything on her own. The Ballet School program won't be possible.'

'Surely you can still audition?' She looked as sad as I felt.

'No. Can you please let them know? I can't – I don't know who to call.' I stared down at the floor, trying not to cry. What good did tears do? They didn't help. 'I'm sorry I let you down. I think I can still come to class on Saturdays, if that's all right.'

'Of course it is. And I'm sure we can still work something out. You're a very talented dancer, Brynna. I'll talk to your mother in a few days, when things have improved, and –'

'No! It'll be fine. Thank you. Please call the School

for me. That's all.' I turned and ran from the studio, before I exploded into a million tiny pieces. At the outer door, Stephanie was just coming in, her fancy white and pink ballet bag over her shoulder. I pushed past her, head down, wanting to get as far away as I possibly could from everything that reminded me of ballet and what I'd just given up.

But Stephanie couldn't resist opening her big mouth. 'You'd better not miss the last class,' she called after me. 'You need all the help you can get.'

I skidded to a stop and swung around. 'You're the one who needs help. Someone should choreograph a nasty ballet just for you.'

As she gaped like a stunned goldfish, I shoved at the outer door and walked into the dull, grey afternoon.

CHAPTER 24

I stood at the bus stop and couldn't help smiling at the way I'd wiped the gloating expression off Stephanie's face. That was the only good thing that had happened all day. Then I thought about Dad lying in the bed like a mummy and realised I'd just given up the audition I'd worked towards for years, and it felt like my heart was being squeezed inside my chest. When the bus came, I could hardly find the energy to climb up the steps and find a seat.

Mum still wasn't home when I got back, so I peeled a heap of potatoes and put them on to cook. There was cold sliced ham in the fridge and frozen peas. That'd have to do. I had no idea what time Mum and Uncle Tony would be home.

Tam slouched into the kitchen. 'Are you cooking?'

'Not really.' I told him what there was to eat. 'Yuck,' he said. 'Can't we get pizza?'

'No, we can't,' Orrin said, coming in behind him. 'You can have ham sandwiches if you don't want vegies.'

Just as the potatoes boiled, Mum and Uncle Tony came in, carrying a big parcel of fish and chips. Mum turned off the boiling pot and we all sat round the table, stuffing our faces. Mum said the scan on Dad's head hadn't shown anything and she and Uncle Tony talked about the words the doctors used – *prognosis fairly good, but we won't know more until he regains consciousness*. Then they added other doctor-type words that made it all sound even worse and I stopped listening. My eyes wanted to close and I wished it was bed-time already.

'Brynna.' Mum was helping me up from the table. 'Come on, clean your teeth and hop into bed.'

'But it's not time yet.'

'Near enough.' She pushed me towards the bathroom and I didn't object. Sleep. That was what I wanted. If I went straight to sleep, I wouldn't have to toss and turn and think about missing the audition. Sounded good to me.

I woke early and lay there, looking out at the trees in the backyard. They were fruit trees and at this time of the year, their bare, grey branches looked like bony arms. Some of them were even bent into ballet positions.

Ballet. I didn't want to think about that. Oh well, it would make Lucy feel better if I wasn't in the special class. Or going for the audition. Would Mum make me go to school today? Did I want to? I kind of did, because the alternative was either hanging round the house all day or hanging round the hospital in the waiting room.

I got up and washed my face, then found a clean bowl

and filled it with corn flakes and milk. I made myself a hot Milo and sat at the table, munching away and watching the clock hands tick round. I heard a groan in the lounge room and Uncle Tony staggered out, scratching his head with both hands, his hair up on end.

'Coffee,' he muttered. 'Got to have coffee.'

He made himself a cup and sat opposite me at the table. 'How ya going, Brynnie?'

'Good.' I kept eating. 'Are we going back to the hospital today?'

'Your mum and I are. I don't know about you kids. She was talking about sending you to school. Except for Tam. He'll have to come with us.'

'School.' Maybe school would be all right, as long as no one asked me what was wrong. 'I'd better get ready then.'

'Ready for what?' Mum asked, shuffling in in her bunny slippers.

'School.'

She sat down next to me and gave me a hug. 'You don't have to go if you don't want to. But it might be better than sitting in that place all day.'

'Mmmm.' I didn't want to say what I really wanted, which was for everything to go back to the way it was two days ago.

'What's this Orrin was telling me about your ballet class?'

I stood up quickly and put my bowl in the sink. 'Don't worry about it. I've talked to Ms Ellergren. It's fine.'

'But we didn't –'

I was out of there before Mum could say any more and the fact that she didn't follow me and want to talk about it told me I was right – she couldn't deal with the extra problem the audition created right now and I'd done the right thing.

It was just that the right thing felt like a huge weight on top of me. But I had to get over it. There would be another chance. If I kept telling myself that, I'd be fine.

What I didn't count on was that Lucy had already heard I'd dropped out, and she was desperate to know why. Probably because she was hoping she'd get my place.

'Is it true?' she asked, grabbing my arm to stop me from walking into class. 'Did you just not turn up last night?'

'Of course I turned up,' I said. 'I talked to Ms Ellergren and everything.'

'But – you weren't in the class. Kate rang me.'

'So?'

'So she said there were only five there last night. And Ms Ellergren wasn't very happy. What happened?'

'Things at home have changed, that's all. Ms Ellergren understands.' It was almost a lie, but I didn't care. And I didn't want to talk about it. I didn't care, didn't care, didn't care. If I just kept saying it, it'd be true. 'Come on, we'll be late.'

Mrs Nguyen smiled at me as I entered the classroom. 'How is your father?' she asked softly.

'They're still waiting. He's still the same.' I hoped

she'd be happy with that. Mum must've rung the school, but I didn't want to explain anything to Mrs Nguyen either. I went and sat down before she could say any more. At recess and lunchtime, I took a book and walked to the furthest end of the school grounds, where I hunched down behind a tree and read, the words blurring as I tried to block out the other kids yelling and running round. I knew Jade and Lucy wouldn't come looking for me.

After school, I got home to find an empty house again and my heart sped up till I found Mum's note on the table. *We're at the hospital. No change. Just visiting. Back at 6. Love Mum.*

More than two hours away. TV was boring. I was sick of reading. *Ricky*. Would he be waiting at the youth hall for me? Or would he let me down again? I wanted him to be there. I desperately needed to see a friendly face. I changed into dancing clothes and put my ballet shoes in a bag, but I doubted I'd be doing any dancing. What was the point? Besides, it just reminded me of what I'd lost, and how pleased Stephanie would be. Maybe Ricky and I could go to the milk bar and have an ice-cream or something.

He was waiting outside the hall, on the wooden bench with only two slats left on it. The others had long been smashed off. 'Hey. Why the long face?'

All day at school, no one except Lucy and Mrs Nguyen had even looked at me properly, let alone noticed how sad I was, yet he'd seen it in two seconds. I wanted to burst into tears, but that would've freaked him right out. I pressed my lips together hard, then said, 'My dad had an accident at work. He's in hospital and he's really bad.'

'Man, that's not cool at all. You must be on a real downer.'

I sat next to him, perching on the slats. 'It's horrible. He just lies there, like he's never going to wake up again.'

'Those ER shows on TV, they say a coma's a good thing, you know.' He mimed putting a stethoscope in his ears and listening for my heartbeat. 'Yep, the heart's good, the brain just needs a bit of rest.'

'Yeah, right.' I smiled at him. 'Dr Ricky to the rescue, huh?'

'For sure. I'm a doctor when I've got time off from being a basketball star.' He nudged me. 'Suppose you don't wanna dance, then?'

'Um –' I thought about it. I could tell he wanted to and I thought it might stop me dwelling on Dad and Ms Ellergren. 'Yeah, why not?'

As we warmed up, I decided to put him in front of me for a change. 'You can show me how to do it,' I said. 'Inspire me.'

'Just call me Ricky Magic Nureyev,' he said, curtseying low. 'The *bell-ay* dancer with the best slam dunk in history.'

A giggle spluttered out of me and, shaking my head, I lined up behind him. This was going to be one bizarre practice session. And it was. He put *Swan Lake* on again and we spent half the time laughing and slapping our hands over our mouths so the bald man wouldn't hear us and throw us out. The other half of the time, Ricky danced whatever he felt like and I followed, copying even his most peculiar dance sequences, some of which had nothing to do with ballet at all. It was such fun and for once my body fell into the music and I responded with my heart first.

We said goodbye at the corner of my street. 'You take it easy, now,' he said. 'Your dad'll be cool. I know these things.'

I shrugged. 'If you say so.' I wished I could believe him, but it seemed like so much had gone wrong lately that was out of my control. I had to keep hoping, but Ricky was no magician. As I got closer to our house, I could hear music blaring – some kind of heavy metal song with clanging guitars and a singer who shouted. The neighbours would be feral. Was it Tam or Orrin?

Orrin. He was in the lounge, doing push-ups while the music deafened him and the windows rattled. Too busy grunting as he bobbed up and down, he didn't see me. I found the volume knob on the player and turned it down.

'What did you do that for?' He collapsed onto his stomach. 'I still had forty to go.'

'You'll have forty neighbours lining up to kill you, more like it.'

'Just a bit of motivation music. Where have you been? Mum rang.'

'I was at the youth hall.' I chewed on a fingernail. 'What did she say?'

'They'll be home soon. We're gonna eat, then go to the hospital.'

I sat down, fast. 'Why? What's wrong?' I had a picture of us all around Dad's bed, getting ready to say goodbye to him, and tried hard to shake it out of my head.

'Nothing. Dad's come to at last, although he still can't talk. They said we can visit him tonight for a while.' He started his push-ups again. 'Forty-one. Forty-two. Turn the music up, will you?'

I did as he asked, only not as loud, and wondered if I should join him. That was what my life had been like lately – up, down, up, down – so push-ups might have helped me. But I had homework to do, to catch up on what I'd missed in class, so I dragged the books out of my bag and sat at the kitchen table. By the time Mum, Tam and Uncle Tony came home, I was finished.

'Brynnie, did Orrin tell you about Dad?' Mum's face was one big smile.

'Yes. That's good news, isn't it? When can he come home?'

'Not for a week or two, probably. But at least he's conscious.' She patted my shoulder. 'Before we go back to the hospital later, you and I need to have a little talk.'

I nodded. This was going to be about the audition, but it was too late. Ms Ellergren would've cancelled my appointment time already. It was too late to fix what I'd done. I was still sick about it, but the horrible feeling was fading just a tiny bit. Maybe one day it would go away.

CHAPTER 25

We ate soup and toasted sandwiches, then while Tam had a shower, Mum and I sat in my bedroom. 'Why did you go and see Ms Ellergren without telling me?' she said.

'I don't know. You were with Dad and I didn't want to bother you. I didn't want to make things worse by you having to worry about ballet stuff.' I stared out the window; I didn't want to look at her face in case I started to cry. 'Ms Ellergren was really nice about it.'

'But you told her you were pulling out of the audition.'

'Yeah, well – I have to. If Dad can't work for a while and you have to look after him when he comes out of hospital, we'll have no money. And there won't be time for me to go to all the program classes.'

'Brynnie, the money is not a problem. Dad's wages will be covered by work insurance. And I certainly don't expect you to give up ballet to help me with housework. That'd be the very last thing I'd want you to do. Housework! Yuck!'

I tried to laugh, but it came out all wobbly. 'But I thought –'

'What?' She took hold of my hand and squeezed it. 'Tell me.'

'I thought Dad was going to die!' A big sob burst out of me and I hated the sound of it. I wanted to be tough and brave, not a wuss.

'Did you think giving up your ballet audition was going to save him?'

'No! Of course not. But it seemed like you and Dad had given up our house and your jobs and everything to come here for me, and I just thought what I wanted was too much. That I had to give something up, to make things balance out again.'

I hadn't really thought about it like that when I'd gone to see Ms Ellergren, but now, as it came out of my mouth, I could see that was exactly how I'd worked it out and why I'd done it.

'What happened to your dad could've happened anywhere. There were times at his job in Bendigo when he could've got hurt, just like now. We might get run over walking down the street, for heaven's sake.' She sighed. 'We all have our own path, you know, our own lives. Things like your dad's accident don't happen because you have big, wonderful things happen in your life. The universe isn't like that.'

I blew my nose, struggling to accept what she'd said. 'But it still affects all of us.'

'Of course it does. But it's not a balancing act. Having something great happen doesn't mean the next thing will be horrible. And remember,' she said, touching the tip of my nose with her finger, 'an accident really is just an accident. Being good enough and working so hard to get ready for the audition is a big achievement, something you did all on your own.'

'Too late now.' My chest hurt and my fingernails dug into my palms. If Mum was serious, it meant I had given up the audition for nothing. I'd lost my place because I told Ms Ellergren I couldn't do it, when it was actually okay. What had I done?

'Of course it's not too late,' Mum said. 'Ms Ellergren rang me last night and talked to me about it. She understood what had happened, and how you thought you were doing the right thing. She hadn't called the NBS to cancel, just in case.'

'What?' I was on a roller-coaster, racing back up to the top, into light again. I couldn't believe it. I could still audition? I jumped off the bed. 'Tell me you're not just saying that to cheer me up. Tell me it's true!'

'It's true.' Mum stood up and cupped my face in her hands. And that was the only thing that stopped me from hopping up and down like a demented frog. 'It's true, and you'll be terrific.'

'Thanks, Mum, thanks a million, million times. You don't know how much this means to me.'

'Oh, I've got a vague idea.' She laughed. 'Now, get changed and let's go and see your dad. If you're lucky, you might even get a smile out of him.'

I pulled off my dance clothes and found some jeans

and a sweatshirt that were reasonably clean, but it was hard to get them on. I felt like electricity was zipping through me, and it made me want to sing and dance and throw myself round the room like a maniac. Except my room was so small that I would have knocked myself out.

Dad was still in the ICU, but his eyes were open. When we went in to see him, I could tell he sensed we were there, but he couldn't see us until we got right to his bed. His head and neck were being held tightly in place. Mum had explained that was because his neck was damaged and had to be supported until it healed more.

He still looked scarily un-Dad to me. Too many tubes and bandages, and he was too still. He focused on me and blinked.

'Hi, Dad,' I said. And then I couldn't think of anything else to say. What did you say? How's the view? All he could see was the ceiling. How are you feeling? He was on big doses of pain-killers so he couldn't feel anything. When are you going to get better? He couldn't answer that. So I just smiled and let Mum take my place.

She held his free hand. 'Hi, Mike, I'm back again.' He blinked twice. 'We're all here this time. Orrin and Tam are over there.' Orrin waved, Tam grinned. 'How are you feeling?'

Dad just blinked a few times.

Mum kept talking, telling him all the things we'd been doing, which wasn't much, but she filled in about ten minutes, along with Uncle Tony chipping in. Then she said,

'It's Brynna's audition on Friday. Won't be long before we can all go and watch her dance on stage.'

The electric feeling came back and I tried hard not to fidget. I'd missed the last class. All that was left now was the audition. Was I ready? I felt like I'd never be ready, ever. I stretched my legs way out and arched my feet, banging against the wall, and pulled them back quickly, hoping no one had noticed.

But Mum had. 'We'll have to go in a minute,' she said. 'Time's nearly up, so you boys had better come and say hello to your dad.'

They shuffled over and muttered a few things to Dad, who blinked. I took Orrin's place by the bed to say goodbye, then Mum shooed us out, but not before I saw tears slide out of the corners of Dad's eyes and down the side of his face. I went back and leant down to give him a kiss on the cheek. 'Hurry up and get better, Dad,' I said. 'We need you.'

He blinked three times at me and his eyes crinkled up a bit. That was the closest he could get to a smile, but it was enough for me. He *was* going to get better! Everything would be okay. It would just take time, like Mum said.

I might as well not have gone to school on Thursday. My brain had moved to another planet and all I could think about was the auditions. The others would be at the School in South Melbourne, getting changed, putting on their ballet shoes, checking their ribbons, smoothing their hair, stretching and warming up.

What would it be like? How many people watched you, judged you? I imagined Stephanie tripping and falling flat on her face, and stopped in case I jinxed myself. Mrs Nguyen must've thought I was still worried about Dad. When she asked me questions and I couldn't answer, because I hadn't been listening, she didn't get mad with me, just moved on to the next person.

At home, I wandered around the house like a lost cloud. I couldn't settle to anything. And just as I'd decided to get out the lino and do some practice, the phone rang.

'Hello.'

'Is that Brynna?'

'Yes.' I didn't recognise the voice.

'I thought you'd like to know the auditions were really hard, and I don't think you're going to be good enough. So maybe you should withdraw now, so you won't embarrass yourself.'

Shock made me dumb for a few seconds. Stephanie! How dare she! Then a cold, brittle anger speared through me like an icicle. 'Obviously you made a complete idiot of yourself, Stephanie, and don't have a hope of getting in.'

She gasped. 'I'm a certainty. Mum said I was. So did Ms Ellergren.'

'Ms Ellergren would never say that to anyone, least of all you.' I wanted to be really nasty to her, as nasty as she was to me, but suddenly I pitied her and that was what popped out of my mouth. 'I feel sorry for you.'

'What? What do you mean?'

I couldn't explain it, so I hung up the phone and found my hand was shaking so much that the receiver rattled. And my stupid brain immediately said, *Maybe she's right. Maybe you should give up now.*

Pain shot through my head and I crouched down against the wall, my arms wrapped around me. *I will not cry, I will not cry, she's not worth it.*

'Whassa matter?' Tam said, crashing past me on his way to the fridge. 'You feeling sick or something?'

'I'm fine,' I mumbled.

Orrin ambled in behind him. 'Brynnie, what's up?'

Why didn't they leave me alone? Then I could crumble and die in peace.

Strong hands lifted me up. Orrin peered into my face. 'Why are you crying? Dad's going to be fine.'

I sniffed. 'I know.'

'Who was that on the phone?'

'Nobody.'

'Garbage.' He sat me down at the table. 'Tam, get her a drink of water.'

A glass of water slopped in front of me.

'What's wrong?' Orrin glanced at Tam. 'We won't leave you alone until you tell us.'

'Stephanie – this girl in my ballet class. She had her audition today.' I sucked in a deep, shuddering breath. 'She called and – she said it was really hard and I wouldn't be good enough, so I might as well pull out now.'

'Is this the same girl who cut up your shoes?'

'How did you know?' I stared at him.

'Mum filled us in,' Tam said. He sat across from me, slouched in the chair. 'So why are you being such a wuss? Tell her to get stuffed.'

'Well, I tried, but –'

'You'll blow them outta the water,' Tam said. 'Stop worrying.'

'I will?'

'Geez, course you will,' he huffed. 'You've got the star factor, like big bro here. I don't know why you're worrying about it, or taking any notice of Miss Snotty.'

'Who says I'm a star?' Orrin snapped.

The last thing I needed was fighting brothers.

'Look, I know I'm a dud,' Tam said. 'Can't play footy, hate the city, no good at school. That's cool.'

'You're not a dud!' I said.

Orrin folded his arms and said, 'Is that why you bolted back to Bendigo? Couldn't stand the pressure of having to make an effort?'

'That's bulldust!' Tam cried, his face flushing. 'I'm just not like you guys, that's all. No one says I have to be.'

'That's right,' said Orrin. 'But no one said you have to use us as an excuse to drop out and be a loser, either.' Now his face was red, too, and his eyes flashed.

'I'm doing fine,' Tam said. 'I'm doing what I want.'

'Which is what? Sponging off Uncle Tony? Getting detention for not doing homework?'

'That was before. We've sorted it out now. I've started

the apprenticeship at the blacksmithing place. Old Teddy says I'm good at it.'

'Are you going to stick at it?' Orrin asked. I hid a grin – he sounded just like Dad.

'Course I am!'

'Good.' He turned to me. 'And you can ignore what Miss Snotty said and focus on getting your head in the right place for tomorrow, okay?'

I saluted. 'Yes, sir!'

'Smarty.' He took a fake swipe at my head and grinned. 'I've got footy training. Brynna needs to work on her audition stuff. So that means you're cooking dinner, Tam.'

'Me?'

'Him?' That was going to be a first and maybe a dangerous one.

'Mum said there are two meat pies in the freezer. Follow the instructions on the packet and peel some spuds. Lots of them. I'm off.'

Tam opened the freezer, grumbling to himself, and I escaped to the garage, but despite what my two brothers had told me, Stephanie's voice echoed inside my head and my practice went badly. When I overbalanced on an arabesque and nearly twisted my ankle, I knew it was time to stop.

Sleep that night was a long time coming. Even visiting Dad and seeing his eyes open, blinking yes and no in response to Mum and feeling him squeeze my hand for luck, hadn't kept up my spirits. I wanted the audition to be over, or I wanted someone to announce that it was cancelled. Anything except having to actually go through with it!

And as for Stephanie – her voice still echoed in my head. I knew she was jealous, but she said the audition was really hard, that I wasn't up to it.

Mrs Calzotti's voice echoed in my mind, something she'd said to me at my last class with her, something I'd ignored at the time, thinking she was being a bit over the top. *Everyone wants to be the prima ballerina, even in dance class. You will meet many dancers who would wish a broken ankle onto you. That is where you will have to learn to be tougher.*

Tam was right. I was being a wuss, letting Stephanie upset me, especially when that had been her whole aim. I punched my pillow into shape and settled down to sleep.

CHAPTER 26

When I woke up on Friday morning, *Audition Day!* flashed in my brain like a neon sign, and I jumped out of bed. The house felt strangely empty, even though it was nearly eight. I heard Orrin and Tam talking, a low rumble through their bedroom wall, but there was no Uncle Tony on the couch in the lounge. And Mum wasn't in her bed either. They'd obviously gone back to the hospital – but why?

The phone on the wall didn't give me an answer. I made myself some toast and hot chocolate for breakfast and sat at the table, trying to force down the toast without much success. My throat was squeezed so tight that even the chocolate made me choke and cough. Finally I gave up and went to pack my bag for the audition. I put on my best leotard and tights, freshly washed – the instructions said to come ready, with warm clothes on top. In my bag went the new shoes that I'd bought, a drink bottle of water, an extra jacket to wear in case I got cold. Then I dressed in warm clothes over my ballet gear, and put my runners on.

My audition was at 11. The clock had sped around

to 9.05 already and Mum still wasn't home. Why didn't she call? I'd have to go to the Ballet School on the bus. What if I caught the wrong one, or there was a traffic jam? Didn't Mum have to be with me at the audition?

When I heard our car in the driveway a couple of minutes later, the relief rolled through me in a huge rush and I had to sit down. Mum burst in through the front door, pulling off her jacket and scarf, her face pale. 'Oh Brynna, I'm sorry. I hope you're all ready.'

'Where were you?' I cried.

'At the hospital. Come on, let's go.' She didn't stop to brush her hair or have breakfast, just grabbed her best black winter coat and headed back to the car. As I followed her, I heard Orrin and Tam yell, 'Good luck!' and it made me smile.

Mum put the car into gear and we roared up our street and around the corner, and were on our way into the city centre. 'Westgate Bridge will be quickest,' she muttered, signaling and changing lanes. I huddled down in my seat, hugging my bag to my chest.

When it seemed that she'd calmed down a bit and was driving slower, I asked, 'Why were you at the hospital so early? Is something wrong with Dad?'

She glanced sideways at me and bit her lip, but said nothing.

'Mum, come on. I can tell you're upset. Keeping it a secret won't make me any less nervous about the audition. It'll make me worse!'

She sighed, a big ragged sigh. 'Your dad's lapsed back into a coma. They had to operate again early this morning. There was a swelling under his skull that could've been a clot and they had to relieve the pressure.'

'Is he going to die?' My voice came out all wobbly.

'No, of course not!' She coughed and sighed again. 'It's something that happens with head injuries – they were on the lookout for it, and they caught it in time, so that's good.'

'But?'

'We have to wait now and trust they'll be able to stop any further – problems.' She checked her watch. 'Goodness, we'd better get a move on! Hope there's parking.'

'There is,' I said. 'The school's got a car park underneath it.'

'That's right,' Mum said. 'Now, Brynna, I know it's going to be hard to focus on the audition with the worry about Dad, but you have to. Dad, of all people, would want you to do your absolute best and succeed. He certainly wouldn't want to think that his being injured meant you – well – stuffed it up.'

'I know.' And I did know she was right, but the dull, leaden feeling was back in my legs and arms and I wondered how I'd even get out of the car, let alone dance. Couldn't I put the audition off till Dad was better? I knew it wasn't possible. I had to go through with it, even if I made a complete mess of it. There was always next year.

It seemed like we parked, went up in the lift and

were at the front desk, being ticked off a list, within about ten seconds. Mum helped me pin numbers on my front and back – 15 – was that lucky or not? I barely had time to look around at the photos and displays before she gave me a big hug and said, 'Knock them dead, Brynnie!' in my ear, and left. I was surrounded by about sixteen girls and a few boys. Most of them seemed smaller than me, although there were some the same height. Instead of chattering, everyone was strangely quiet, sneaking glances at each other and making faces.

A few minutes later, a woman came and led us through a glass door and down a long hall; I hardly had time to stare around me, but I glimpsed a classroom with some computers in it, and a little room with exercise bikes and drink machines. The woman showed us a long row of photos on the wall, and pointed to two of them. 'This is who will be assessing you today,' she said. 'Ms Ballantyne and Ms Carr.' I sucked in my breath. I recognised both of them – they were famous! Ms Ballantyne was the Director of the Ballet School. My heart skittered in my chest and I put my hand over it to try and calm it down.

We stopped in front of a set of white double doors. 'This is Studio Three,' she said. 'You can all go in now and warm up. Don't be nervous. You'll be fine.' She gave us a big smile and ushered us in.

'Don't be nervous, you'll be fine.' Who was she kidding? My legs had gone from lead to jelly, but I tottered into the studio, took my jacket and shoes off and put them in one of the pigeonholes. I closed my eyes and tried deep breathing, visualising Ms Ellergren smiling at me, but it didn't work. All that I could see was Dad lying in the hospital bed with his eyes closed, machines beeping. I didn't want him to die!

I swallowed hard, past the lump in my throat and went to the barre against the wall to start my warm-up. Stretch, bend, flex, stretch, bend, flex. The studio wasn't as big as I expected and I could hear the others whispering and giggling around me. Stretch, bend, flex – how were my arms? Oops, there I was – the mirrored wall was right in front of me and I hadn't even noticed it! Yes, arms looked okay, even if they felt jerky. Back straight, head up. Focus, I had to focus.

Right then, instead of seeing Dad in the hospital bed, unconscious, I saw him the day he came to help me at the youth hall, watching me from the doorway and clapping. 'Lovely,' he'd said, and his face had been glowing.

'Lovely,' I whispered to myself. 'For Dad.'

'Is everyone ready?' a voice said.

I quickly took my track pants off, stowed them away, turned and smiled. Even the sight of two elegant women sitting behind a table on the other side of the room, gazing at us, only made me waver for a couple of seconds. Then I stepped forward, my mind calm, my body fizzing lightly with energy.

It was now or never!

I'm not sure what I expected – complicated dance routines? Gruelling tests? Instead, it was just like a normal class. A man with an accent was our teacher and he was incredibly patient, taking us through familiar exercises, watching and directing. We were all trying to keep clear of each other, trying not to copy – or I was, at least. If I was going to make any mistakes, they'd be my own! The piano boomed out the notes, the woman playing it focused on watching the teacher and waiting for instructions.

Finally, after nearly an hour, the class had finished. Then we lined up and were each closely examined by either Ms Ballantyne or Ms Carr. I stood in front of Ms Ballantyne, as straight as I could, not sure if the sweat trickling down my back was from the class or my nerves. She asked me to stretch and bend, looking at parts of my body, getting me to turn my hips out to test rotation, and checking my insteps and my Achilles tendons. After each part, she'd tick a box on the form in front of her. Finally she smiled and said, 'Thank you, Brynna, we'll be in touch.'

Suddenly the audition was over. Some of the others were still lining up for their physical examination, but I was free to go. I felt as light as a cloud, taking off my shoes and my numbers, putting on my jacket, drifting out along the corridor. The world seemed unreal, fuzzy around the edges and incredibly bright and clear in front of me. When I found Mum waiting in the reception area, I had to blink a few times to make sure she was actually there.

'How did it go?' she asked, her eyebrows raised high, her face expectant.

'Good – I think.' I held my hands out wide. 'I've done it. I can't undo it now. I just have to keep my fingers and toes and everything else crossed.'

'Don't do that,' she said, grinning. 'We won't find out for a while yet.'

'I won't be able to wait!' How did anyone stand the not knowing? Did your life just stop until the letter arrived?

'It'll pass before you know it. Let's head home and then I'm going back to the hospital.' As she pressed the button for the lift, the reality of Dad in a coma crashed down on me again. I wrapped my jacket tightly around me, stared down at my feet, back in their pink and white runners. I'd done my best; now Dad had to do his.

CHAPTER 27

It was too late to go to school. Once I would've loved being able to hang round at home, watching TV and reading, but my brain was like a crazy movie camera, playing bits of the audition over and over. Mum had gone back to the hospital, but she wouldn't let any of us go with her, saying that we'd only get in the way. She promised to call if anything changed.

Orrin and Tam went for a run and then lay around the lounge room, watching DVDs they'd rented from a nearby video shop. The constant explosions and car chases with squealing tyres nearly drove me insane and when it was close to four, I changed into my ballet gear again and set off for the youth hall. I knew Ricky wouldn't be there and I planned to ask one of the TV boys to help me with the tables, but they were already folded against the wall.

I put on my new shoes and ran my hand over the soft leather, wondering if these would be my lucky shoes, the ones I could say helped me get into the NBS. I shook my head. Mum was right. It'd be ages before I found out and by then these shoes might be all worn out and no longer special.

Rap, rap! I jumped at the noise and looked up. It was Ricky, tapping on the window and waving at me. I slid the window open and he climbed in. 'Hey, what's happening?' he said.

'Practice,' I said. 'I thought you'd given up ballet for basketball.'

'Ha,' he scoffed. 'What's the point of training? Even though I made the guys go through it all and work superhard. Our so-called coach hasn't turned up all week. So much for the big talk about faith in ourselves, eh?'

I poked him hard in the chest. 'Watch it. You're talking about my mum. She happens to be your so-called coach.' I ignored the astonishment on his face and snapped, 'I told you, my dad nearly died in an accident at work, and coaching you guys hasn't exactly been top of Mum's list. And now he might –' My voice quavered and I couldn't say another word. I bit down hard on my lip and turned away.

The silence stretched out for several long seconds and then he said, 'I'm sorry. I didn't know. Nobody did. We just, you know, we didn't know what to think.'

I turned back. He stood there with his arms folded and couldn't meet my eyes. 'I guess it's not your fault,' I said. 'It's been horrible and I had to do my audition today, even though Dad's still on the danger list.'

'It was today?' He whistled through his teeth. 'That musta been majorly hard.'

'Yeah, well –' I couldn't bear another silence, so I flung my arms out. 'So – are we dancing or not?'

'Sure!' He rummaged in his backpack and brought

out his iPod and little speakers. 'I found this new music that sounded cool.' As he fiddled with setting it all up, he said offhandedly, 'Hey, it's our first game tomorrow. I know your mum maybe can't come, or maybe you can't come either, but I thought I'd see – if you wanted to. But you don't have to.'

'Is it at the high school gym?'

'Yeah. Two-thirty. No big deal.'

But I knew it was. His face was pink, even his ears were pink! Ricky might have liked dancing with me, but his first and biggest passion was definitely basketball. I promised myself that I'd do everything I could to be there and I crossed my fingers that Mum could, too. I was sure she wouldn't have forgotten about them, but the week had been – hideous, for all of us, especially her.

Ricky's music boomed out across the room. 'What on earth's that?' I said and he laughed.

'It's cool, hey? It's called the *1812 Overture*. Listen to those cannons. It sounds like a battle charge. I can do some of those big jumps to this.'

'Yes, but you don't want to break a leg before your game, do you?'

His face fell. 'Oh. I suppose not.'

I grinned. 'Let's warm up first, and then we'll see.'

When I got back home, Mum was there, cooking dinner and talking to Tam as he lounged against the sink. 'How's Dad?' I said.

'The same.' Mum sighed and tipped potatoes out of a bag. They thumped onto the bench and rolled into the sink.

Tam glanced at me. 'Mum says you didn't let Miss Snotty upset you.'

'Why didn't you say anything?' she asked.

I shrugged. 'It wasn't worth it. I want to know how come you didn't tell your basketball team why you couldn't go to training.'

'I did.' She frowned. 'I rang the man who organised the gym. You mean he didn't pass the message on?' She opened the oven door and poked at the chicken, then banged it shut again. 'That's a disaster. They'll think I don't care, that I've let them down.' Her breath huffed out and she looked at me. 'How did you know?'

'Ricky told me. They did think that. And their first game's tomorrow.'

'Of course it is. And I'll bet they haven't done any of the training stuff I showed them.' She sat down at the table, head in hands. 'I feel terrible!'

'They've been training,' I said. 'Ricky made them.'

'You're kidding,' she said and a big smile spread across her face. 'That's fantastic. I'll get on the phone straight after dinner and call them all to apologise and explain.'

'Why wait?' Tam said. 'We can manage spuds and stuff.'

Mum leapt up and gave him a big hug, then rushed off with the phone to find her players list. Tam was all flushed, his eyes bright. 'Right, you can do carrots, Brynnie,' he said.

'Yes, sir, kitchen patrol, sir!' I laughed.

By eight o'clock, my eyelids were drooping and Mum sent me off to bed, where I crashed into a deep, dark sleep for nearly twelve hours. Even when I woke the next morning, I didn't feel rested. I felt flat. I gazed up at the ceiling, wondering where the emotions of yesterday had all gone. The audition seemed like a dream.

I shot up in bed – it was Saturday! Ballet class. The audition no longer loomed. It was back to normal and Ms Ellergren would surely expect me to be there. Or would she? Mum was humming in the kitchen, banging plates and cutlery onto the table. As I joined her, she said, 'You're not ready for class. Better get a move on.' That answered my question.

When we reached the studio, she told me, 'I'll drop you off and then go to the hospital. Hopefully, there'll be better news today. If I'm not here when class is over, just wait, okay?'

I nodded and checked my watch. I was late. I threw off my clothes in the changing room and rushed into the studio, ballet shoes dangling from my hand, and sat in a corner to put them on. For once, Ms Ellergren didn't reprimand me, just carried on with the class and I joined in at the back, ignoring curious glances from some of the others. The class was a disaster. I stumbled, overbalanced, nearly fell, and each time my face burned with embarrassment until I stopped caring. So I was having a very bad day. So what? I shut out the Silhouettes' sniggers and Ms Ellergren's frown and waited for the class to end, then locked myself in the toilet until I was sure everyone had left.

Everyone except Ms Ellergren. She was waiting outside for me and I checked her expression, but she didn't look mad, or even disappointed. Instead, she smiled. 'How is your father?' she asked.

I shrugged. 'Not good. He's – he's in a coma again.' I swallowed hard, looking away.

'I'm sorry.' She paused. 'So how was the audition?'

Her voice had a funny catch in it and I stared up at her. Her eyes were bright, her eyebrows lifted like Mum's. She really wanted to know!

'It was good. I think.' I grinned.

'I'm sure you did well,' she said warmly. 'You realise if they contact you in the next week to come in for a full physical screening that means you've got a conditional place.'

'Really?' I squeaked. 'I thought we had to wait for ages. But conditional on what?'

She laughed. 'The physical screening. But I'm sure you'll pass that with flying colours.'

'Oh.' It was too much to take in. Conditional offer? I might hear in a week? I'd been trying so hard to put it out of my head and Ms Ellergren had dumped it right back in again.

'Your mum will be waiting,' she said. 'Do let me know if you hear anything, won't you?'

I nodded, left in a daze and found Mum outside in the car, all ready to go to her basketball game. Thank goodness there was something to distract me again!

The high school gym was almost empty, with a few parents dotted round the seating and the two teams bunched up, one at each end. I found a place to sit; Mum joined her team and got straight into the pep talk, waving her hands round. I watched Ricky and the other boys, their eyes focused totally on her, nodding as she gave instructions. The referee blew his whistle and the game was on.

At first, Ricky's team was outplayed all over the court and within five minutes they were down twelve points. Some of the boys drooped, disheartened, but Ricky rallied them, and Mum walked up and down the sideline, shouting encouragement. Suddenly Ricky had the ball and virtually floated down the court, dribbling and swerving, dodging round opposition players. I almost expected him to do a couple of grands jetés! Instead, he jumped, lobbed the ball and it soared into the air and down through the hoop.

I jumped up, cheering and clapping and when he realised it was me, he gave a little bow. Then he was back into the game again, focused and urging the others on. Every time he turned or twisted, jumped or ran, I saw the same grace and flow that he danced with. It was like magic. I decided I wasn't going to give up on trying to persuade him to do a ballet class – even if basketball was his passion, dancing would just add to what he already had.

In the end, his team lost, keeping up but never quite catching the other team's twelve-point lead from the beginning, but when I joined them afterwards, I could tell they were overjoyed to get that close. 'The others are the second-top team,' Mum told them. 'You did fantastically well. Another few training sessions and you'll blitz them next time.' When she saw them glancing at each other, she added, 'And I won't let you down again. If a disaster happens, I'll get Brynna to call you all and let you know. I promise.'

'That's cool,' Ricky said, grinning at me.

After saying goodbye, Mum and I raced down Ballarat Road to catch the last twenty minutes of Orrin's game, then we all went to the hospital to see Dad. As we entered the ward, a nurse pulled Mum aside, her face serious. We three bunched together, silently watching Mum's face. What was the nurse telling her? I didn't realise I was holding my breath until Mum smiled, then it whooshed out of me and I felt Tam's hands on my shoulders.

Mum came over to us. 'He's conscious again at last.' Her chin trembled and she took a shaky breath. 'We can see him for two minutes, that's all.'

Tears stung my eyes as we shuffled into Dad's room. He looked more like a mummified statue than ever, but at least the machines were beeping at a regular pace. We stood round his bed and took turns at saying hi, keeping our voices low. Same as before, he could hardly move, but his eyes followed us and crinkled up at the corners a lot, and he could squeeze our hands pretty hard. I kept getting a big lump in my throat and having to check my shoelaces until it went away again.

Uncle Tony had gone back to work, leaving Tam to stay for a bit longer, so it was the four of us on Saturday night.

Or so I thought, until Orrin confessed that he was going to the movies with a girl.

'A girl?' Tam said, astonished. 'Who'd want to go out with you?'

Orrin blushed an amazing shade of beetroot and went off to find a clean T-shirt to wear with his best jeans, while Mum sat at the table, making notes about her game plans for her team and Tam and I watched TV. Everything felt like it was getting back to normal, but every now and then I'd think about the audition and whether they'd call me, and my heart would make a big thump in my chest. The only solution was to make myself focus on the normal stuff, and block the NBS out of my head. And that seemed impossible!

CHAPTER 28

It was the longest week of my life! Every day dragged, from the time I woke up until the time I lay down again in the dark and tried to go to sleep. I felt like a robot at first, stiff and mechanical, as if the past few days had drained me of all my blood and energy. We visited Dad every night and gradually he had less and less machinery attached to him. By Thursday, he was sitting up and had the tube out of his mouth, but he still couldn't talk much. The nurse said the tube would have hurt his throat and it would take a while to settle down. Whenever we went into his room, his whole face lit up, and that made us all really happy too.

On Wednesday night, Tam went back to Bendigo with Uncle Tony, who'd come down to see Dad again. Mum said Tam was missing too much school, so even though he grumbled, in the end he seemed okay about it. Probably he was bored being home alone every day, although he was never going to admit it. It was sad seeing him leave again, but at least this time we said goodbye properly.

School was like an ocean for me. I was just one more

fish swimming around, hiding behind seaweed and drifting along with friends like Lala. Jade ignored me completely, which was fine by me. Who wanted to hang with a shark? Lucy was nice to me, but once she saw I'd made friends with Lala, she left me and went off with Jade. That was fine by me, too. I had dance practice with Ricky, but no more special classes with Ms Ellergren. I missed them – they'd given me the total focus on perfection that I'd wanted. Maybe one day I'd be able to afford private lessons.

I refused to think about the National Ballet School. If I did, I'd go crazy. It didn't stop me from lifting the receiver and checking that our phone still worked every day when I got home from school, as if maybe Mum hadn't paid the bill! Then I'd find something else to do and stay as far away from the phone as I could.

On Friday afternoon, before I went to meet Ricky at the youth hall, I searched for one of my favourite books on ballet, to show him photos from *The Nutcracker* and *The Firebird*. Photos where there were lots of male dancers doing amazing leaps! I thought maybe it was in my room, but when I couldn't find it, I went out to the freezing garage to check in the last few boxes of stuff we hadn't unpacked yet.

'Brynna! Brynna!' Orrin shouted out the back door, loud enough for neighbours three streets away to hear.

'What?' As I came out of the garage, he laughed.

'You've got black dust all over your face.'

'Gee, thanks. What do you want?'

'Phone for you.'

My heart stopped, just like that, and for a few seconds I couldn't hear anything. Then the sound of traffic and birds and someone's radio playing burst back in full volume. 'What?' I said, stupidly.

He shook his head and pointed back into the kitchen. 'Better hurry before she hangs up.'

She. So it wasn't Ricky. And he would've said if it had been Mum. I tried to get up the back steps, but my legs were so shaky that I nearly fell. Orrin grabbed my arm and hauled me inside, muttering, 'What is your *problem*?' Then something clicked and he grinned at me. 'You gonna be long?'

Energy zapped through me and I ran for the phone, picked it up and said too loudly, 'Hello?'

'Is that Brynna Davies?' It was a woman's voice, quiet, gracious.

'Yes,' I squeaked.

'It's Ms Ballantyne here, Brynna. From the National Ballet School. How are you?'

I was dying here in my kitchen, but I tried to sound normal. 'Good, thanks.'

'I'm calling about your audition. We were very happy with you, and we'd like you to come in next Tuesday for a full physical screening. Would that be possible?'

'Yes.' Not an intelligent answer, but she didn't seem to mind.

'Good. Let's say four-thirty, after school?'

'Yes.'

'You realise this means we are making you a conditional offer of a place in the part-time program?' Now she was starting to sound a bit worried that I wasn't listening properly, or wasn't taking her seriously. I sucked in a calming breath and made my shoulders relax.

'Yes, Ms Ellergren explained it. I'll tell Mum.' I hesitated, then it burst out of me. 'Thank you so much. You don't know what this means to me.'

'It's an important time for you, Brynna. We are going to be very happy to have you as a student. I'm sure you'll do wonderfully. Goodbye.'

'Thank you. Bye.'

My hands were shaking so much that I dropped the phone twice before I got it back on the cradle. Orrin was right behind me. 'Well?'

I jumped and spun round, gave him a big poke in the ribs, then danced round the kitchen table. 'I've done it! I'm in! I've got a place!'

'I guess you're happy then,' he said, grinning.

'Happy? I am – in rapture!' I shouted.

The front door opened and Mum came in. 'What's all the shouting? I could hear you out in the street.' She took one look at my face and said, 'Oh, Brynnie, you did it, didn't you?' Her face looked like it did when she told me about Dad, and I stopped dancing.

'What's the matter? Is Dad – ?'

'No, he's fine.' She started to cry, but then she was laughing and waving her hands around. 'I can't believe it – yes, I can. It's amazing. You're amazing. Both of you are amazing. We're all amazing!'

She gathered Orrin and me into a big hug, and he groaned, but he hugged back just as hard as I did. 'Just wait till we tell your dad,' she said.

I couldn't wait to tell Ricky! I wanted to tell the whole world, actually, but Dad and Ricky were the most important. Stephanie and Lucy no longer mattered.

And even though I knew Dad and Ricky and Tam would be happy for me, just like Mum and Orrin, even though I'd proved that the moving house and the new schools and jobs were worth it – in the end, like Mum said, it all came back to me. I had proved to myself that I had the talent and dedication and guts it took to be a ballerina. And that was what counted.

ACKNOWLEDGEMENTS

There have been many people who helped me with research for this book, but in particular I want to thank: Moira McAlister, who sparked the original idea; Christine Bowman at the West Pointe Ballet Academy; and Leigh Rowles, Head of Student Training at The Australian Ballet School.